RIVER OF BONES

AN ANNA KRONBERG MYSTERY

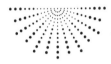

ANNELIE WENDEBERG

Editing: Tom Welch

Cover Design: Nuno Moreira

ALL YOU NEED TO KNOW...

To those who have hung out with me since my (terribly unprofessional) beginnings as an author.

This is for you.

PROLOGUE

Boston, September 1893

*H*ad Mr Wilbur known that his two Dachshunds would resurrect a corpse, he certainly wouldn't have taken them for a walk.

He would have stayed in bed.

It was a crisp Sunday morning when Mr Wilbur strolled down Middlesex Avenue and into the marshes of Mystic River. The grass stood high. Dew was rubbing off on his new trousers, moisture creeping through cotton, weighing them down. He should have taken the time to put on his wellingtons, he told himself. Or his gaiters, at the very least.

A thin sheet of fog hovered above the water, tickled by rays of sunlight. Mr Wilbur thought of fairies. He shook his head. Ridiculous. He turned, his eyes searching for his dogs. Their sleek bodies were hidden by the grass, their tails pointing straight up, flicking like whips. When they began yipping in excitement, he wondered what they'd found. He would have to ask the maid to wash them upon his return — they were surely rolling in something revolting.

The yipping grew more frantic as Mr Wilbur stepped out onto the bank. He regretted the move instantly as his shoes sank into the soft mud. With a curse, he took two steps back, and skidded his mucky soles over clumps of grass. Then he lifted his head to call his dogs back.

And paused.

There was a big lump lying on the bank, fifteen yards or so away. The dogs were doing...*what* precisely? Tugging at something? Eating it? What was it, anyway? He narrowed his eyes. It was large. As large as a fat man. Shaped like one, too. No, that was impossible.

He would make an appointment with his ophthalmologist. Yes, right away. No, it was Sunday. That would have to wait until tomorrow.

Mr Wilbur lifted his fingers to his mouth and whistled. The dogs didn't even look up. They were entirely focused on...whatever that thing was.

He felt anger roll in his belly. Disobedience would not be toler—

A sharp, aggressive bark — like a small cannon shot. The dogs scattered like fleas.

The lump gave a violent twitch.

A wail cut through the fog.

Yours is the light by which my spirit's born. You are my sun, my moon, and all my stars.

   E. E. Cummings

The Boston Post, *Tuesday, September 5, 1893*

CORONER'S NOTICE - Body of a man found two days ago at Mystic River near Middlesex Avenue, Somerville: about 45 years old, 5 feet 9 inches in height, stout build, dark hair, smooth face; had on Kentucky jean pants, brown vest, light calico shirt, blue cotton socks, and congress gaiters. Body at City Morgue for identification. Henry Millers, M.D. & Jacob Rubenstein, Coroners.

~

*B*y midsummer 1893, the recession had begun to grind people down. The census reported surging unemployment rates, and panic was beginning to stir among the working class. Housing prices notched up every other week, and the slums grew more and more crowded.

During that time of economic upheaval, only three things kept Margery from fearing the four of us would surely fall into poverty: her ability to preserve nearly everything she found at the farmer's market, a rather extensive root cellar for storing unfathomable amounts of food for months (never mind that this wasn't a root cellar at all, but a tunnel and secret escape route), and my inheritance that was mostly in gold.

I had told Margery and Zachary that I had inherited more than seventy thousand dollars, which they trusted would be enough for a lifetime. Had I told them the truth of it, Margery would have fallen over in shock.

Now, with autumn approaching, Margery, Zach, and Klara were going to the market almost daily. They would set out after breakfast and return before lunch, their small hand-cart laden with whatever was being sold at the best price that day. Then they'd sort their loot in the kitchen. Our tunnel was equipped with two rows of shelves down its consider-able length, holding jars of fruits, jams, tomatoes, applesauce, artichokes, casks of sauerkraut and pickles, and even wheels of cheese sealed with cotton cloth and butter. Come winter, our larder would be stocked with ham, bacon, smoked sausages, crocks of lard, and other delicacies.

Margery seemed to be preparing for war. Or the apocalypse.

When the others went to market, I would make my way to Wards Six and Seven. It was a world of stink, grime, rats, dead goats, and drunkards. For that stink, I'd quit my lecturing post at the medical school for women. I'd closed my practice for these drunkards. And I hadn't been happier in years.

If anyone had asked what had compelled this choice, I'm not sure I would have found a satisfying answer. Slum life isn't pretty; everyone knows that. But what I found nearly impossible to stomach were the countless drunken children and babies.

In the slums, alcohol makes life bearable. In stale beer dives, the dregs from old casks were gathered and rounds of beer were sold at two cents. The recession hadn't changed that in the least, and the slum dwellers kept on drinking savagely. To them, alcohol was an anaesthetic. It lifted any and all inhibitions. It wiped away worries. Consequences no longer existed. People coupled, made babies. Pregnancies were a mere afterthought. Births happened nearly accidentally for mothers so stone drunk they didn't even feel the contractions. If both mother and child survived, the father or one of the older siblings would often wrap up the newcomer in some dirty rag to dump it in a park or an alleyway, or on the doorstep of some fashionable house.

Most of those babies ended up in squalid almshouses, with paupers, drunks, and the insane for company. They slept and cried and shat in small cardboard boxes lined with cotton wool, their lifespans measured in days.

My daughter seemed to have inherited my impulse to try to fix hopeless situations. She kept bringing home dying animals. Songbirds and their chicks that she'd wrenched from the maw of a cat, horribly chewed up but still twitching. Sickly kittens that were only skin and bone, and much too small to survive without their mother. And once, a small dog that must have been purposely set on fire. They all died. It was heartbreaking to watch Klara trying her best, and failing. I did all I could to help her care for them, but she needed to understand that sometimes, all one could do was to make a passing more bearable.

She had a thousand questions, but asked none of them. She rarely spoke a word.

Margery couldn't fathom why I frequented Boston's worst slums, why I wanted to help the dregs, the ignorant, the shiftless. Zach, though, understood without me ever needing to explain.

Once you open your eyes to the suffering around you, it's nearly impossible to ever shut them again.

But one day, my trip to the slums was forestalled by a knock at the front door.

'Good day, Dr Arlington.' Inspector McCurley ripped off his hat, and straightened his mop of unruly hair with several impatient flicks of his hand.

It took me a moment to process his appearance. I hadn't seen him for three months. Not since shortly after he and I killed Haywood — the man who had murdered three women and was known as the Railway Strangler.

McCurley looked healthier. Happier. A light shone in his blue eyes that hadn't been there before.

'Is your daughter well?' I asked.

He smiled broadly. 'She's crawling.' And then his eyes flared with a mix of pride and fear. 'She's horrifyingly fast.'

I chuckled. 'Ha! Wait until she starts walking. *That* is most terrifying. They wobble around on chubby legs and their huge head seems to take aim at every pointy bit of furniture nearby.'

His shoulders dropped. I regretted my words a little. As a police inspector, he must have seen enough blood and gore to know how a toddler with a head wound would look.

Clearing his throat, he pushed his hands into his pockets. 'I've come to ask a favour. For your help, really. You'll be paid for your time, of course...' He trailed off, glanced over my shoulder and spotted Klara, who was getting ready to leave with Zach and Margery. 'She has grown so much.'

'Sometimes I could swear she grows half an inch overnight. Why don't you come in, Inspector?' I said, stepping aside.

We walked toward the sitting room, but he said, 'I'd like to talk to you in private. In your office, perhaps?'

'Of course.' Steering us into my office, I wondered what he might want.

He shut the door, and cleared his throat. 'Early this morning, a body was found on the bank of Mystic River in Somerville.'

I propped my hip against the edge of my desk. 'And you've been assigned the case, which allows only one conclusion.'

He inclined his head. 'First evidence points to homicide. An autopsy is scheduled for...' He looked around the room, then pulled a watch from his pocket. 'An hour and a half from now. But that's not why I'm calling on you. A boy was found huddled with the corpse. Maybe six or seven years old — we're not sure. He's malnourished. Skittish as a cornered rabbit. The police surgeon described him as disturbed and unresponsive.'

'He examined the boy?'

'Well...from a distance. More or less. The boy wouldn't let the man touch him. He began screaming when the surgeon tried to pull him up. It was the strangest sound. Like a tortured animal.' McCurley shrugged helplessly. 'He's covered in grime and reeks of decomposition.'

'Did he say anything?'

'Not a word.'

I chewed on the inside of my cheek. 'And he is your only witness to a possible crime?'

A brief nod.

'You think I could get him to talk?'

'I've seen you work with children—'

'Babies,' I corrected him.

'Babies, their fathers, wet-nurses and sons of wet-nurses.' He gave me smirk. 'Every time you came to visit, it felt

7

like we'd learned how to breathe again. Even Ms Hacker ceased fidgeting. You have a way of making even the wariest people trust you.' He came to a sudden halt. Blood rose to his ears.

His reaction puzzled me. I knew him as an unreadable man, who held his emotions on a very short leash.

'Is the boy aggressive?'

'Aggressive? No, not as far as I can see. He sits hunched in a corner for the most part. He doesn't react when spoken to. When someone tries to touch him, he screams. But he doesn't lash out. He makes himself smaller, if that's even possible. It's obvious that the boy is terrified.'

'Hum.' I pushed away from my desk, glanced at my doctor's bag, wondering whether I would need it, but grabbed it just in case. As we left the office, a thought struck me. 'Just a moment.' I dashed into my bedroom, found coloured pens and paper and Klara's illustrated book on exotic birds, and stuffed them into my bag. Then I went into the garden, looking for my daughter.

Zach was pulling the handcart out from the toolshed, and Klara was busy picking strawberries. Her lips and cheeks were red with berry juice. There was a smudge of dirt above her eyebrow.

'Would you like to go on an adventure with me?' I asked.

At the word "adventure," she perked up. She grinned and a strawberry nearly dropped from her mouth. She stuffed it back in with her knuckles.

'I need to go to the police station to talk to a boy. I think I might need your help.' I held out my hand to her, and then called to Zachary, 'You don't need her to steer the chariot, do you?'

Zach blinked down at the handcart, snorted, and waved me off with a shake of his head.

Klara gathered her apron in one hand and grasped a seam

of my knickerbockers in the other. McCurley looked at us, about to ask a question, but then dropped it.

As the police carriage was driving us to Headquarters at Pemberton Square, McCurley interjected, 'You look well.'

'Thank you. You, too.'

His gaze slid from me to Klara, who was stuffing strawberry after strawberry into her mouth.

I bumped her gently with my elbow. 'Leave two or three for the boy. The Inspector said he's skinny.'

Klara stopped chewing, her cheeks bulging, eyebrows raised. She swallowed, gave me a small nod, and gazed down at the strawberries in her lap. She counted out three in her left hand and, after a brief paused, added another two. Then she gathered the rest in her right hand and shoved them into her face.

'The boy is not in a cell, is he?' I asked McCurley.

'He's in my office. Boyle is keeping an eye on him.'

We alighted, entered Headquarters, and climbed a flight of stairs to McCurley's office. He knocked once, then pushed the door open. Boyle, sitting inside next to the door, nodded in greeting and tipped his hat. A thick wave of odours hit me. The office stank of river muck and decomposition. I peeked into the room and spied a boy squeezed under McCurley's desk. His clothes were in tatters. His skin was so entirely covered in dirt that one couldn't even be sure if a boy or a girl was hidden underneath the grime.

We entered. McCurley dismissed Sergeant Boyle. The boy's gaze was stuck to the legs of the chair Boyle had vacated, and that McCurley now occupied.

Klara and I sat down on the floor, a short distance from the desk. The boy sat on his haunches, the fingers of one hand splayed against the floorboards, eyes glued to McCurley's shoes. Only twice did his gaze dart toward my daughter and me.

9

I opened my bag, pulled out the pencils, paper, and book, and pushed them all to Klara. Then I sat back and watched. The boy did not move. But his attention was dragged away from McCurley's shoes to the sheets of paper Klara had arranged in front of herself. She placed a row of strawberries on one sheet, and began to draw on the other. A tree, a flower, a butterfly.

As though shocked by his audacity to find himself staring at the colourful things laid out in front of him, the boy's eyes flared, and then squeezed shut just before he pressed his face against his knees.

Klara looked from him to me, frowning. She picked up the strawberries, held them out to me, and cocked her head toward the boy.

'Just a moment,' I said softly to her, and then to the boy, 'Would you like strawberries? They are from our garden. Klara picked them for you.'

There was no reaction.

'What is your name? Mine is Elizabeth.'

Still no reaction.

I tapped a finger on one of Klara's pens, rolling it in his direction. And then another. They bopped against his threadbare boots. He lifted his head a fraction to peek through his bangs. Sharp hazel eyes held mine for a brief moment. A tremor went through him, and he scooted back an inch, away from the offending pencils.

I rolled another toward him. He frowned at it, then up at me.

'Would you like a strawberry?' I asked.

Instantly, his gaze dropped to my lips.

And very slowly, I repeated my question.

He swallowed.

I nodded at my daughter. 'I think you can offer one to him now.'

In a flash, her small fist shot forward, her fingers uncurled to present slightly mushed berries. The boy didn't move, didn't unfasten his gaze from Klara's outstretched hand. She scooted a little closer, and a little closer yet.

His hand crept forward.

Unceremoniously, Klara dumped the berries on his palm.

He stared at them, stunned.

I said, 'They are yours.' When he did not react, I waved my hand in front of my face to draw his attention, and spoke slowly, 'They are yours. You can eat them. If you like straw-berries.'

And one by one, he picked them from his hand and conveyed them to his mouth. All the while, there was nothing but fear in his expression. That of a dog who'd been kicked too often.

I tapped a finger to my mouth. 'You see what I say?'

He licked his lips.

A finger to my ear. 'You don't hear what I say?'

He dropped his gaze.

I turned to McCurley and leant my cheek against my hand so that the boy couldn't read my lips. 'Would you make a loud noise, please? I'd like to test a theory.'

He stood, lifted his chair and sat it down with force. At the harsh *clonk*, the boy's gaze shot up to where chair legs had met floorboards. Nervously, he scanned us for clues. I smiled at him and motioned toward his left hand that was still splayed on the floor. 'You listen with your fingers. You are very smart.'

A brief, unintended smile flitted across his features. Then he pressed his face back against his knees.

'McCurley, the boy is deaf. I don't know if anyone has taught him sign language, but I think if he knew it, he would have used it by now.'

'There's a school for deaf children only a few blocks from

here,' McCurley replied. 'I will call for someone to try to talk to him. Sign to him. Perhaps, they can take him in for a few days until we find his family.'

'Hum. What did the police surgeon recommend?'

McCurley hesitated. 'Are you sure the boy can't hear us?'

'Yes. Very sure.' I eyed the boy from the corner of my vision as he watched Klara draw a picture of what seemed to be Zach.

McCurley exhaled. 'If I can't find an alternative by the end of the day, the police surgeon will transfer the boy to an asylum for children.'

'What kind of solution is *that* supposed to be? The boy is *terrified*. He trusts no one. He needs company, a warm bath, new clothes, food, and rest. Not a cell and a cold shower.'

'The surgeon tried to have him bathed. There was…quite a ruckus.'

'Well, so far we're doing well.' I turned back to the boy, and tapped my lips with my fingers. He knew the gesture well enough now. 'You need a bath.'

His face darkened and he looked away.

Klara pushed her book toward him. When he didn't react, she picked it up and shoved it against his shins. The boy scooted back.

'Do you want him to have it?' I asked her. She nodded. 'As a present?' She nodded more.

I wiggled my fingers in front of my face to catch the boy's attention. 'Klara wants you to have the book. It's yours, if you want it.'

He stared at her for several long moments, then reached out and picked the book from her outstretched hands. With reverence, he opened it, caressed its pages, traced the illustrations of exotic birds, the colours of their plumage leaping from the paper. Klara inched closer, tapped his hand and rubbed a finger over his skin.

He froze, looked at the grimy back of his hand, turned it over to expose an even dirtier palm and wrist. A nervous glance bounced between me, Klara, and McCurley. The boy snapped the book shut and pushed it back to my daughter.

Klara snatched the boy's fingers and pulled.

Confused and desperate, he squinted at me.

'You can have a warm bath and new clothes. And then food.'

At that, his stomach yowled.

'You can keep the book. It's a present.'

And that was all it took.

McCurley walked ahead, then came Klara still holding the boy's hand. I followed. Part of me feared the boy would snap and strike Klara. He was teetering on a dangerous edge.

'There *is* warm water, isn't there?' I asked McCurley.

'Of course. We have a circulation boiler installed for the common bathroom and the kitchens of the two boarding rooms upstairs.'

We entered the bathroom, and I began filling a tub with warm water from the tap, and found a bar of soap and a brush. The boy unbuttoned the remnants of his shirt. He threw glances from beneath his bangs to McCurley who sat on a stool by the door, seemingly immersed in a newspaper, and at Klara who sat by McCurley's feet and stared up at him, puzzling over his silence.

'Do you want the Inspector to leave?' I asked.

He shrugged, pulled off his shoes, and shed a pair of trousers that merely reached down to his knees. He folded everything neatly on a pile atop his boots. Then he stepped into the tub, all bone and skin and grime. Stiffly, he folded himself into it, picked up the soap, and sniffed at it.

'He needs clothes,' I said to McCurley.

'Boyle's arranged some. I'll go get them.'

When McCurley returned with a stack of clean secondhand clothes and a pair of boots, the boy had scrubbed off most of the grey layers that had covered his skin and hair. Nearly clean, his skin didn't look much better. Signs of scabies, ringworm, and impetigo were visible from a distance. And I was sure his mop of wet brown hair was home to hundreds of lice.

Hoping to at least reduce the number of itch mites, I asked the boy to lather up once more, then turned to McCurley. 'Burn everything he wore. He's crawling with mites and has a variety of skin infections.'

McCurley sucked air through his teeth. 'The medical examiner needs to look at them first.'

'Then touch them only with a fire poker.'

'You think he's from the slums?'

'I don't know. Have you seen his knees and elbows?'

'They are calloused.'

'Yes. Is there a mine nearby?'

McCurley narrowed his eyes at the boy. 'The Butte & Boston copper mine. But child labour has just been abolished. The factories are all inspected regularly. Anyone who employs children under fourteen is fined. Which doesn't really mean a thing to some.' Then he scratched his neck and added, 'I need to question the boy. It can't wait any longer. The trail is getting cold.'

2

I stepped off the omnibus and weaved my way up Hanover Street. It was unusually warm for September, which was extending the diarrhoeal season beyond what was normal. It usually started in June and ended in mid-August, killing thousands of babies among the destitute and hopeless. Mothers had no idea what to do with a wailing skeleton of a baby, and even when I told them what precautions they should take, they were often too resigned and discouraged to take them. Sometimes I wondered if this was hell. But I've never believed in the deities and their games.

The stink of old sweat and urine, decomposing goat and pig carcasses, and faeces stood thick in the air. I turned left, away from the Black Sea district, and the squalor took on a new dimension. The hopelessness, the entire lack of ambition of the mostly Irish population, was stunning. So much worse than what I'd experienced in London's St Giles.

Again, I wondered if the boy from Mystic River had grown up here. It worried me that he was on constant alert and hadn't replied to any of McCurley's questions — all simple enough to be answered with A nod or a shake of the head. But the boy had only retreated farther and farther into his silent shell.

He was intelligent, that much was obvious. I saw nothing in him that reminded me of the many slum children who had been fed their first beer before they could even walk. There was a sharp mind behind those terrified hazel eyes, and I could only guess what had been done to him.

I hoped that McCurley had found a place for him, that the boy hadn't spent the night in the Inspector's office or in a holding cell.

I nearly stumbled over the stiff legs of a dead goat, distracted by a dozen children playing ball with a bundle of rags, tied together with string. Their goal was marked by two groups of drunks sitting slumped on the pavement, their backs propped against a wall. Other drunks lay flat on the ground, sleeping or unconscious. I scanned their faces in passing for signs of infectious disease — typhus, measles, smallpox. Finding none, I neared the wharves, where a heap of dozing children were guarded by three women, who nervously paced the perimeter. One tried to get a youngster to drink from a mug. White mourning cloths hung from nearly every window in the surrounding buildings.

I stopped at a distance of several paces, and announced that I was a physician and there to help. One of the mothers muffled a cry and made to embrace me, but I held up my hands, pulled a handkerchief up around my mouth and nose, made sure my hair was all tucked into a second handkerchief around my head, and then set to work. After a few brief questions, palpitating the children's chests and abdomens, listening to their hacking coughs, examining their rashes, and taking their temperatures, it became clear that they all had typhus. Their grimy hair was crawling with lice, their scalps covered in scabs.

The youngest child was dying.

I looked up at one of the women. 'How many have died already, and when?'

'Started two weeks ago. The babes went first.' She wiped her nose.

'How many?' I repeated.

'Half a dozen.'

'Did the Board of Health send anyone?'

Behind me, another woman snorted. 'There was two young fellas sent. They walked all through that house.' She waved at the building in front of us. 'And into that'n over there. They wrote something into their little notebooks, and left. Didn't even ask a question.' She hiked the girdle of her skirts higher up and spat on the ground.

Sighing, I nodded. 'Fetch a bucket of water, a few rags, and...' I caught myself before I said *beer*. 'And get cold tea. Wrap a wet cloth around each child's calves and ankles to bring down the fever. They need to drink lots of liquids. And take them out of the sun, but make sure they get fresh air.'

A low-pitched, rough whistling noise sounded from the entrance of the alley. A watchman came running up, his police whistle bouncing around his neck. 'You!' he called out and pointed in our direction. The women slunk back into the house. The watchman's gaze remained stuck on me. Panting, he slithered to a halt.

I pulled the handkerchief from my face. 'Is there a problem?'

'You are arrested!'

I gaped as he pulled a pair of manacles from his belt. 'May I ask for what?'

'Attempted killing.'

'Wha—' I was cut off by an elbow to my side. The manacles came down on my wrists. 'Are you mad?'

'Stop resisting!' He jerked so hard on my arms that I

feared he'd break my wrists. On instinct, I manoeuvred my body to lessen the pain but accidentally bumped my head against the man's chin.

He retaliated with a fist to my face, and then I snapped. I was fully aware that I shouldn't have called him 'prick,' and perhaps I should not have stomped my heel on is toes, but…

I WOKE IN A CELL. A stone floor had sucked all warmth from my prone body. My face was stuck to someone's stinky boots. I lifted my head and looked up at the person whose feet I'd used as a pillow, and found a woman slumped on a bench, drool running from her half-open mouth.

Gingerly, I moved to a sitting position and was surprised that I was able to keep my food down. That idiot policeman had given me a headache that rivalled the pounding of a jackhammer.

'Hello?' I called through the barred door. 'This is Dr Elizabeth Arlington. I believe I was arrested by mistake.'

Ha! How many people claim exactly that after waking up in a cell? Probably every single one of them. 'Hello?'

No response.

I sat back down and put my throbbing head in my hands.

An hour or so later, someone walked up the corridor to the cells. I scrambled up and peeked through the bars. 'Excuse me.'

The man who'd arrested me appeared. A sneer was plastered on his face.

'Why was I arrested?'

'Told you why. You nearly killed a man.'

'And when was that, if I may ask?'

'Couple of days ago. You threw a man down the stairs of his own home.'

'I…what?'

'A health inspector witnessed it and reported you to the police.'

It dawned on me. I had helped deliver a baby in Ward Six. The father was stone drunk, toppled about the room, and kept attacking me. I had to get rid of him. So I let him chase me out of the room. Then I bopped his chin. He staggered a few steps back and tumbled down the stairs. I'd had better things to do than tend to the goose egg on his head.

'Your health inspector was mistaken. A drunkard attacked me while I was helping his wife deliver their baby.'

The watchman looked me up and down, and said, 'You probably offered yourself to him for a beer, the way you look.'

'Thanks to you, cockchafer,' I pressed through my teeth.

He clonked his nightstick against the bars and showed me his teeth. 'Want me to teach you what that mouth of yours is for, wench?'

For a brief moment, I did consider luring him into my cell and taking him down. Unfortunately, no one would believe my version of events. And simple protest wouldn't get me anywhere with this man. So I opted for acting. I let my shoulders droop, turned away, and muttered, 'Inspector McCurley will probably give you a medal.'

'What did you say?'

I waved a hand at him. 'Nothing.'

'Did you say McCurley? Inspector McCurley? Is he looking for you?'

Sitting down next to the half-conscious woman who smelled like she had taken a swim in the sewers, I crossed my arms over my chest, and muttered, 'I'm not saying anything about that knucklehead McCurley. I want a lawyer.'

He flashed a grin. 'Well, well, *well.*' He said and disappeared.

It was almost too easy.

It didn't take long for McCurley to arrive. He glanced through the bars, and slowly turned back to the watchman. 'Open the cell.' His voice sounded amiable, but I heard the grit beneath the softness.

The watchman unlocked the door, and McCurley strode up to me. I remained seated, not sure what his plans were. His eyes lingered on mine for longer than necessary. He filled his lungs, turned around, and approached the watchman. 'Just to make sure I understood you correctly: An inspector from the Board of Health reported that Dr Elizabeth Arlington had attempted to kill a man in Ward Six?'

The watchman nodded.

'An officer was sent to her home at once, of course.'

'We... I...' was all the watchman managed.

'And the Bureau of Criminal Investigation was notified of the attempted killing.'

'Erm...'

'Ah, I see. The case was given to *you*.' McCurley spoke in a tone that implied the watchman was utterly brilliant, and thus, assigned the case.

'It appears so.' The man cleared his throat, blind to the trap he was stepping into.

'A report was filed, of course.'

Here, the watchman gave a small shrug, and McCurley's control snapped. He grabbed the man by the front of his uniform, lifted him clean off his feet and slammed him against the bars. Quite the feat. The watchman was not only heavier than McCurley, he was also two inches or so taller.

'Hooper, I swear I'll stuff your head through the bars if you don't tell me what precisely the health inspector said, and who set you on this ridiculous errand!'

'He...he...'

'I want the name of the man!' barked McCurley. His voice

could have cut glass. I was glad I wasn't on the receiving end of his wrath.

'Jeffries,' the watchman squeaked. 'It was Jeffries! He said he heard someone say that she pushed a man down the stairs. He was unconscious for hours. He could have died!'

McCurley set Hooper back on his feet. 'Where was that?'

'At...at Clarks.'

'Most everyone is unconscious at Clarks! They are all hopelessly drunk. They all topple down the stairs when going off to their beer dive. Don't tell me you don't know that! What problem does this Jeffries have with Dr Arlington?'

Despite the ruckus McCurley was making, the woman next to me continued snoring merrily.

'Because she's a troublemaker. Who knows what she gets for *helping* that hopeless scum!' Hooper hissed, emphasising the word *helping* as if the word were a cockroach that needed crushing under his boot.

'I might be able to explain that,' I said, and both men looked at me as though I'd just materialised. 'Jeffries and the other inspectors the Board of Health sends to Wards Six and Seven don't report on infant deaths or infectious disease. They take fifty dollars each month for keeping quiet about the dire situation in the slums. I report every death and illness I observe. Without anyone asking me or paying me to do so. It makes the health inspectors *and* the Board look rather...bad.'

McCurley screwed his eyes shut, and snarled, 'And how did you come by that fabulous black eye?'

'She resisted arrest,' Hooper volunteered. Talking wasn't his forte. The man should be keeping his mouth shut. Permanently.

'I resisted getting my wrists fractured. Watchman Cooper

applied unnecessary force. I was already shackled when I got this.' I pointed at my eye.

McCurley took in the watchman's entirely unbruised face, and said softly, 'May I borrow your manacles for a moment?'

The man found himself shackled and carted off in a heartbeat.

'WOULD you like to freshen up a bit before a police carriage drives you home?' McCurley asked on the way from the holding cells out into the street.

The sudden brightness hurt my eyes. Something dark was moving in my periphery. I blinked, and turned my head. The twitching dark blob moved with me. 'No, I'd much rather retrieve my doctor's bag. If it still exists, that is. I lost it when Hooper accosted me.'

'Where?'

'Fleet Street.' I untied the two handkerchiefs and shook them out, then used them to slap at my clothes.

'What are you doing?'

'I was treating a group of children with typhus. They were infested with lice. I'm just making sure I get rid of most of the critters.'

'I'll accompany you,' McCurley said, matter-of-factly.

'Whatever for?'

'To make up for all my stupid, arrogant, and corrupt colleagues.' He was still seething. A few months back I'd told him my opinion of the police: stupid, arrogant, and corrupt. It seemed he agreed. McCurley was one of the few exceptions.

'Don't fuss, McCurley. Fleet Street isn't far from here, I'm not seriously injured, and a policeman at my side won't help matters much.'

'How would they know I'm a policeman? I'm not wearing a uniform. In fact, I rarely am, in case you haven't noticed.'

'But everyone knows you are a police inspector.'

'All the better. The drunks won't dare attack you.' He came to a halt and motioned in the direction of the slums. 'Why are you doing this? Why put yourself in danger?'

I shrugged, and walked on. Every step jostled my brain.

'I can't imagine the slum dwellers are paying you much.'

'I'm not asking them for money.' I reached Hanover Street and increased my tempo. The dark thing in the corner of my vision grew. Stupid Watchman Hooper must have given me a concussion.

'You want to get rid of me,' McCurley observed.

'I want to stop your barrage of questions.'

'My concern is justified.'

We entered Fleet Street and found the same group of children guarded by the same three women. They had a bucket and wet rags, but instead of tea, they were giving them beer. It did not surprise me.

McCurley was my silent shadow as I re-tied the handkerchiefs around my head and face, and stepped up to the huddled group of coughing and moaning children. The youngest had no pulse. I pulled up a bluish eyelid and tapped her eyeball. There was no reaction.

'She is dead,' I said to the women, and got defeated nods in return. McCurley bunched the brim of his hat in his fist, his expression that of a man who was nursing an old knife wound.

'You haven't seen my bag, have you?' I quietly asked no one in particular.

'It's in my room,' one of the women said with a trace of reluctance, then led me up a narrow set of creaking stairs. McCurley followed and I was glad of it. My vision was growing increasingly unsteady. Nausea crept up my throat.

The room was home to many. I counted nine pallets. One was occupied by three children. They were all sick. I examined them, but they weren't as bad off as the ones outside.

'Why have you put the others out on the street?' I asked.

'They'd jus' make the others sick.' She pointed at the children on the pallet.

'They *all* have typhus. Bring the other children back up.'

She grunted, 'Yes, ma'am,' and handed me my bag. It was considerably lighter, but I refrained from opening it and checking its contents. As McCurley and I were turning to leave, she tied a strip of white fabric to the window frame. The mourning cloth hung limply in the stale breeze.

I felt nothing but exhaustion. My capacity for grief was used up.

'Give me your bag,' McCurley said on the dark stairwell, holding out his hand.

I shook my head. I always grew more stubborn when I wasn't feeling well.

'Then give me your hand. It's slippery here. The steps are rotten.'

I put my hand in his and we walked down slowly, he descending a step ahead of me, grasping the mouldy wall for lack of a banister.

Halfway down, one of the steps gave way and my footing slipped. McCurley threw out an arm, blocking me from falling. He steadied me and set me back on my feet.

He frowned. Nodded upstairs. 'Why are you helping them?'

Mute, I shrugged again.

There was something in his expression that gave me pause. Was it disappointment?

I exhaled a sigh. 'I don't know how you can even ask me this. The mortality here is twenty per cent. Twenty of every hundred people die early of hunger and disease! And no one cares. *No one.* One of the most squalid tenement houses in Ward Seven is owned and kept by a prominent member of the Board of Health. He doesn't give a damn, either. All that our government officials have to say about this is, "We need better immigration control!" or "Slums need to be demolished because they are a breeding place for evil!" The Bureau of Statistics of Labor and the Board of Health regularly send men into Wards Six and Seven to classify the occupations of the population and assign health status. They count and describe and file away the lives of thousands of people, but only after thoroughly prettifying their data. And then they discuss the fate of these people in meetings, and issue reports of their own efforts for the newspapers. But is any good ever done? Is anything accomplished? Never! Did you see the sheer number of mourning cloths?' Furious, I thrust my fist toward the room behind us and regretted the movement instantly. The stairwell seemed to tilt away from me.

Lids at half-mast, eyes unfocused, McCurley nodded. 'This is the way I grew up. In a slum just like this. Worse than this, even. New York's Lower East Side. Drunks everywhere. Babies born alcoholics. Children drinking gin from milk bottles.'

I was speechless. 'How did you escape?'

'My mother didn't touch a drop. I guess that's what saved me and my siblings. In the beginning, anyway.' He took another slow step down the stairs and stopped. I leant my shoulder against the wall.

'It all changed when our father...' He cleared his throat. 'That's what we were supposed to call him. I can't be sure if he fathered any of us. Our lives took a turn when he... He wasn't violent, not like others, who beat their wives and children. He mostly just dozed and mumbled and soiled himself. One day he swung a poker at a man who wasn't there. A man he'd made up in his alcohol-addled mind. The hook got stuck in Mother's temple. He snored as she died. I took my sisters and my brother away that day. My brother was only a babe. He was the first to die.'

A muscle in McCurley's temple bounced. 'If we'd had someone like you, my siblings might have survived. So don't let anyone — least of all a man like Hooper — tell you that what you are doing is hopeless.'

He tore himself away and into the sweltering stink of Fleet Street.

With a heavy heart, I stepped onto the pavement and looked up. Something…wasn't…right. I stumbled to a halt. Dropped my bag.

McCurley turned and watched me trying to make sense of my surroundings. The old woman sitting in a doorway mending a shirt. The scrawl of chalk on a window sash. The ball made of rags. It all felt strangely familiar, but…

'I need to go home,' I croaked.

'Are you feeling unwell? You're as white as a sheet.'

'I… I don't know where I am.'

3

*M*cCurley was grinding his teeth all the way from Ward Six to City Hospital, and from there to Savin Hill. I didn't need to turn my head to see it. Tension was rolling off him in waves, despite my repeated reassurances that my concussion wasn't serious, that I definitely did not need to see a doctor, and that my sense of location had been muddled for only a few minutes.

He ignored every single one of my protests.

Still, I was shocked by my condition. I'd never experienced an entire loss of orientation before. My surroundings had felt familiar. Strongly so. But I had somehow…misplaced the map.

'How is the boy?' I asked by way of distraction.

'He is well,' he said, as he helped me climb out of the hansom cab.

'You aren't telling me something.'

His expression shuttered.

'Dammit, McCurley!' I yanked my bag from his arm with a little too much force and teetered sideways. 'Tell me how the boy is, or else I'll imagine he is suffering horribly.'

He scanned me with narrowed eyes. 'If I was a doctor and all my patients were as pigheaded as you, I wouldn't be able to stop myself from shooting a hole in the knee of every one of them.' He curled his arm around my waist. 'Ten steps to your house, probably fifteen to your bed. Walk. Now.'

'You are an ogre!' I growled and put one foot in front of the other. It took some focus, but I managed to reach the house without tripping.

McCurley pushed open the door, and called into the hallway, 'Hello?'

The clanking and bustling noises from the kitchen stopped. McCurley deposited me in Margery's capable hands with the words, 'She has a concussion. The doctor ordered her to stay in bed for two days. Make sure she does.'

'You've seen a doctor?' Margery eyed me from head to toe. 'Never thought I'd see the day.'

'I insisted,' McCurley supplied, and then turned to me. 'I'll tell you about the boy tomorrow.' With that, he left.

Margery pushed out her chin. 'Did you run into another band of ruffians?'

'No. I was arrested. And now I need a bath. I'm crawling with lice.'

'I KNEW you wouldn't stay in bed,' McCurley said when he found me the next afternoon sitting at the kitchen table, pitting plums with Klara. Margery was washing jars. Zach stirred a pot of simmering cranberries. Rather suspicious. Margery would never ask him to help with the cooking, or even light the range for her. I was sure she'd told him to stay nearby in case I needed to be hogtied and carried back to bed.

I tipped an imaginary hat to McCurley. 'I was bored out

of my mind. And my head is perfectly well. Sit. There's a knife. Pits go in here, plums over there.'

Klara was giving him a toothy grin, pointing to knife, bowl with pits, and pot with plum halves as I spoke.

He sat, and got to work.

'Dare I ask what Hooper is doing?' I said.

'Suspended. How is the head?'

'Fine. As I already said. How is the boy?'

Zach cleared his throat and demonstratively knocked a wooden spoon against the side of the large cranberry pot. Margery set a clean jar down with a loud *clonk*. Both seemed a little...vexed? Puzzled, I regarded first them and then McCurley. 'Er... Can I offer you tea or...something?'

'No, thank you.' He stuffed a plum into his mouth.

I kept staring at him until he dropped his gaze and continued cutting plums in half.

'The boy,' I reminded him.

He cleared his throat. 'A teacher from the school for deaf children tried to communicate with him in sign language but told me that the boy doesn't seem to know it. Nor can he write or read. There was nothing about him or his clothes that would tell us where he came from. I tried to show him a map, but he wouldn't even look at it.'

'What about the corpse?'

'Unidentified white male, around forty-five years old. The post-mortem has been postponed to Friday. The medical examiners are still...' McCurley threw a glance around the room, and lowered his voice, '...degassing him. With a lancet. He suffered extensive internal injuries.'

'The post-mortem surgeon knows that without cutting him open? Was the man beaten to death?'

McCurley shook his head. 'It appears he fell from a great height. The gaping wound at the back of his head did him in. Most likely.'

'Any signs he was pushed?'

He shrugged. 'The state of the body is…'

Klara focused at McCurley with utmost interest.

'Basically, he is one big bruise. And…rather…ripe.'

'Maggots?' I asked quietly, and received a nod. 'He's been dead for a week or two?'

'A week, perhaps.'

Zach cleared his throat again. Margery finished clonking the jars around, and said sharply, 'There will be no such talk in *my* kitchen.'

I couldn't hide a grin. 'My apologies.' After risking a quick look at the back of her head, I added, 'But decomposition is a natural process. Zachary's compost heap is doing the exact same thing.'

Zach froze. He threw me a glance that begged me to leave him out of this. Margery slapped a dishtowel against the edge of the sink, whirled around, and propped a fist on her hip. 'Elizabeth Arlington, there are *several* natural processes I do not *ever* wish to have discussed in my kitchen.'

The corner of Zach's mouth curled. Hastily, he turned away to hide a smile from his wife.

'All right,' I said innocently, turned to McCurley and pointed at the plum in his hand. 'That shouldn't go into our preserve.'

He frowned. 'It's only a worm. And it's tiny.'

'Actually, it's a butterfly larva. And putting it into the preserve would be disgusting.'

'You find *this* disgusting, but not a decomp—' A glance from Margery shut him up. 'Still only a worm,' he muttered and flicked it expertly into the bowl with the pits.

'It's not a worm. It's an arthropod, not an annelid. Those are two entirely different phyla.'

McCurley placed down his knife, eyebrows tilted. 'Are they now.'

'It has been so for millennia. I am right and you are wrong, and you know it.'

'It happens every once in a while.' He calmly continued pitting plums.

After several long moments of trying not to laugh, I said, 'I assume an inspector of the Boston Police Department doesn't offer his excellent plum-pitting skills merely to talk about a witness. You came here to ask me something.'

Margery interrupted. 'Hurry up over there. The cranberries are nearly ready to go into the jars.'

I peeked into the large basket that stood on the table. The bottom was still covered with a layer or two of fruits. 'Another ten minutes, I reckon.' Then I turned to McCurley. 'Am I right?'

He grinned and shook his head. 'Indeed, M'lady, it is as you say.' Then he turned somber. 'I need to question the boy, but obviously, that's…quite problematic. I was hoping you would help me. But what bothers me is… He needs a place to live until we find his family. I enquired at the Boston School for Deaf Children. They can only take in five boarders and are already full. But they agreed to put the boy up with the others for the time being. I left him there last night, but they returned him to Headquarters early this morning. At *four* o'clock, as the sergeant told me. The headmaster claimed the boy had misbehaved and would no longer be tolerated. I found him in a cell, curled up in the farthest corner, howling. It took me the best part of the morning to get him to my home. He can stay for a few days while I try to find an alternative. But since the recession…' McCurley sank against the backrest. Groaning, he raked a hand through his hair. 'Orphanages, asylums, almshouses, workhouses — *everything* is overcrowded.'

'If you put him in any of those, he'll never recover.'

'I know that.' McCurley went back to slicing plums. 'The

boy is terrified. Too terrified to give me the information I need to find out where he came from, what happened to him, and who the man is he was found with. There were no papers, no wallet, no valuables or anything else on the body, or on the boy, that could help identify them. And I need to know what he saw.'

'Why can't he stay at your place?'

McCurley pulled in a breath, and methodically gutted plum after plum. 'The landlord has increased the rent, and seeing that there's another tenant, now he wants even more. I asked that the guardianship for the boy be transferred from the Boston Police Department to me. That helps with the budget, but it won't be enough.'

'What's up with that boy?' Margery asked.

'He was found next to a corpse,' McCurley said. 'He's deaf, malnourished, and he's experienced severe hardship. He's scared of people. Not children, though. I got the feeling he wants to protect Billy and Líadáin from me.'

'We will take him in.'

I opened my mouth and clicked it shut. Margery's stance was decisive. Spine straight, shoulders thrown back, chin up. Gooseflesh prickled across my body. She was not a woman who would randomly take in orphans. She wasn't even good with children. Or people in general. She was a person who always stood high up on the battlements of her soul castle, scanning for threats. Ready to shoot whoever dared approach. And now she was practically rolling down her drawbridge for a stranger.

Suddenly, all eyes were on me. Blinking, I sat back. 'You want me to shelter the boy and *interrogate* on him?'

McCurley held up a hand. 'No. It wouldn't cross my mind to ask that of you. I need your help just to ask him simple questions. My plan was to... Well, I guess I ran out of plans. He can live with me for now. I'll find a solution.'

'The top floor is empty,' Zachary murmured.

I grunted. I had no problem with offering the boy a home. There was only one thing... 'If we take in the boy, you must agree to share every bit of information with me. I'll need to read your case notes. I'll need to know your theories, even the wild ones you'd never write down. I'll need to know involved the boy is in the death of that man, and whether I am putting my family in danger. You know what happened the last time I attracted the attention of a murderer.'

'A small boy can't be a murderer!' Margery snapped.

'Of course not. But what if the man *was* killed, and the boy saw it happen? We have to consider the risks.'

'Officially, the boy is living with me. I won't give anyone your address if you take him in.'

'We did say that already, didn't we?' Margery snapped her apron straight and elbowed her husband.

'We'll take him,' Zach said quickly.

McCurley waited for my nod, then dipped his head. His shoulders sagged in relief. 'I don't know what to say.'

'You could say something about the case. Share information.' I suggested with a smile.

He smiled back. 'You and I will meet regularly to discuss the progress of the investigation. And I will inform Professor Goodman right away that you will be witnessing the upcoming examinations of the body.'

Surprised, I lifted an eyebrow. That was fast. 'I can't tell you how much I'm looking forward to it.'

That caused some consternation. 'What?'

I shrugged. 'Postmortems are endlessly fascinating.' Then I turned to Klara. 'Looks like the boy from the police station might come to live with us. What do you think?'

She beamed.

I clapped my hands together. 'All right, then. We take the boy until his family is found. Margery can use some help with the preserves anyway. Hum…' I popped a plum into my mouth, planning the next steps.

'He can sleep in the annex,' Margery said. 'I'll set up a bed.'

I nodded. 'I'd like to see him before we move him here. He's been pushed around a lot. I want to make sure we aren't entirely overwhelming him.'

'What are you suggesting?' McCurley asked.

'I'll pay you a visit this afternoon and examine the two babies. It will show him that I don't mean anyone harm, and it might also give me an idea why he wants to protect them. I planned on checking on Líadáin's hip anyway.'

'Last plum.' McCurley chucked the gutted fruit into the bowl with all the others.

'Let's talk in my office for a moment.'

WITH MY CLUTTERED desk between us, I regarded McCurley for a moment. 'There are hundreds of homeless boys in Boston, yet you are personally invested in this one. Why?'

Frowning, he folded his hands in his lap. 'My instincts tell me he went through a lot. Yet he hasn't been broken by it.'

'But maybe he's about to be.'

'Yes.' He tipped his head to the side, scanning my face. 'Sometimes we meet people we understand instantly. Without ever needing to say a word.'

For a moment, I wasn't sure if he meant the boy or me. I watched him drop his gaze. After a moment, I said, 'Silence never makes you uncomfortable.'

'Silence is merely the lack of noise. Rarely a lack of information.'

'True.'

'The Boston Police Department will pay you a monthly allowance—'

'I don't need it.'

'But... You quit your lecturer post, didn't you? I don't mean to intrude, but is it because of what Haywood did to you?'

'Lecturing didn't suit me any longer.' I didn't elaborate.

'And you closed your practice. Don't you need the money?'

Was there worry in his voice? 'No, I don't need it.'

Nodding, he began to fumble with his hat.

'My reason is...not easy to explain. I used to live in a London slum. It was by choice, but also by necessity. On the one hand, I needed to remain anonymous. On the other, I wanted to use my skills to help people. I told my neighbours that I was a nurse. You can imagine that I never ran out of patients.' I dropped my gaze to my hands, searching for the right words. 'I've been living in Boston for three years now. All the patients I've had could afford to see me. But very few really needed me. My students didn't need me either. Anyone can fill these posts. But the people in Wards Six and Seven? There is no one else.' I looked up at him.

He brushed his fingertips over his moustache. Traced the chaos of papers on my desk with his gaze. 'Do you think you owe me this?'

'Owe you what?'

'To take in the boy. To tell me about yourself. Because of...that night.'

'When you saved my life? I never thanked you for it, Inspector McCurley. Thank you. If you had not broken down my back door and killed Haywood, my daughter would be growing up without a mother.' The memory of that night still haunted me: Haywood's hands around my throat; his weight crushing my windpipe; the cruel words he'd whispered. 'I do owe you. But that's not the reason I told you this small bit about my past. It's more that I...have come to think of you more as...a friend, than a policeman.' And in my mind,

I added, *Two people can't walk a knife's edge hand in hand without being welded together by it or cut apart.*

His expression darkened. His throat worked. 'You don't owe me anything. You helped me catch a killer, and you helped my daughter.'

'I owe you respect and honesty.'

He inclined his head. 'As I owe you.' He paused, then added, 'My friends call me Quinn.'

His offer took me by surprise. I made an effort to harden my expression and keep the corners of my mouth down. 'I'm German. We Germans never address each other with our given names. Only spouses do, and then only *after* the wedding night.'

Shock flared across his features. 'I didn't mean to—'

I clapped a palm over my mouth, bursting with laughter. 'My friends call me Liz. Except the ones I annoy all the time. Those call me Elizabeth.' I held out my hand to him.

A thin smile spread across his face. An eyebrow flicked up lazily. 'So you *are* German. Not British, as your passport states. The Consulate told me exactly that.'

My hand wilted. All warmth escaped my limbs. He'd dug around in my past three months ago. He'd even told me about it and demanded answers. His Chief Superintendent had ordered McCurley to stop meddling after he received a missive from the British Foreign Office. However *that* had come about. McCurley knew his curiosity was threatening my safety and that of my daughter. I curled my hand to a fist. 'You *promised* not to—'

Throwing back his head, he barked a laugh. 'Got you.' Still chuckling, he wiped a hand over his face, and extended the other to me, 'Elizabeth it is, then. I'm always only Quinn, whether I make people cross with me or not.'

I narrowed my eyes at him. 'I guess I have to get used to you having humour. A wicked one at that.'

'Please don't. The joke was an outlier. I'm usually dead serious.'

I blew out a breath. 'I'm relieved. I'd rather talk about decomposing corpses.'

He pulled a cigarette from his breast pocket and tapped its end against the desk.

'Margery will bash your head in with the skillet if you smoke this in the house.'

'I stopped. It's a waste of money. Smoking, that is.' He didn't look at me.

A lump formed in my throat. The recession must have hit him hard. He couldn't afford to keep the boy, couldn't afford to pay for such a small thing as tobacco. I wondered if his pay was lower than that of his fellow inspectors because he was Irish, without an influential family, and thus considered *cheap labour.*

A few more taps of cigarette against desk before he lifted his eyes. 'As I said earlier, the man must have fallen from a great height. Third or fourth floor, the medical examiner told me. He fell on his back, and was moved within the hour. The body was kept curled on its left side for about a week. We don't know where yet. A specialist has begun examining the fly larvae. The corpse has been washed and stuck with a lancet to let the gases escape. Professor Goodman is concerned the body will burst if it is cut open too soon. So far, they've only looked for injuries and the like. Scars that could help identify him. Wounds that might speak to the cause of death. By Friday, he'll be sufficiently degassed to be opened. Goodman will be able to give you more details.'

As I listened to him, I couldn't help but wonder why he was offering me his friendship. During the early summer weeks, when he'd been working on solving a string of murders, he treated me like dirt under his fingernails. I'd been a suspect, and his strategy to get me to talk had been that of a hammer pounding a nail. Only when it had become absolutely necessary, had he allowed me a glimpse behind his aloof facade. I'd seen kindness there. Strength. But also self-doubt and grief. If what he'd revealed was his real self, I'd known him for barely a day. But I would never forget how he saved me from the Railway Strangler, how he helped me suck breath through my damaged windpipe. As though he and I, breathing together, was the most natural thing on earth.

'You told me the body was found by the river. Were there any footprints in the muck? Wheel tracks?' I kept thinking of him as Inspector McCurley and had to correct myself.

'We found both. The body must have been transported in a horse carriage. A four-wheeler. We found the boot prints of two people who moved the corpse from the carriage to the river. It seems that the boy was clinging to the back of the carriage, and dropped off when it slowed down. His prints appeared several yards from where the carriage stopped, and trailed off to a hiding spot in the tall grass, then straight to the corpse.'

'Hum. Did he walk around the body, lean in to search it, or go anywhere else?'

'No. He went straight to the body and laid down next to it.'

'He knew the man was dead,' I said.

Quinn lifted a shoulder. 'The stink was impossible to miss. We captured all prints with Plaster of Paris, including those of the horses and the wheels, of the man who discovered the corpse, his dogs, and the first policeman to arrive at the scene.

'There were no other prints?'

'No, we were lucky. The flood had pushed the river waters up and washed away all earlier footprints. The body was deposited when the tide was lowest and no passersby had yet come up to the river. This and the tide lines gave us a good estimate on when the man was dumped there. About two hours before dawn.'

'Did anyone see the carriage arrive or leave?'

He shook his head.

'Why would someone drop a corpse by the river just after the tide went out? And leave a map of footprints for the police to find?'

'I was asking myself these same questions.'

4

*I*t was Ms Hacker with little Billy clamped under her arm who opened the door to Quinn's apartment. 'The boy is hiding behind the couch,' she whispered and rolled her eyes.

'You've fattened him up well,' I said with a nod to her son.

'He's a good eater, that one.' A smile flitted across her face.

'No problems with breastfeeding?'

'No. Thanks to you. Give me that.' She made an impatient gesture at my jacket.

Before she could take it, I dropped the garment on a peg by the door, kicked off my shoes and stepped into the sitting room. Two windows stood open to ease the late summer heat. The mourning cloths had been removed from the few pictures that hung on the walls. The photograph of Quinn's late wife stood on the mantelpiece without black ribbons framing her likeness. Only three months earlier, this place had been shrouded in grief.

The door to Quinn's bedroom was ajar. 'Just a moment!'

he called through it. He was rummaging around with something, while Líadáin burbled away happily.

I turned to Ms Hacker. 'I'd like to examine the boy, but he won't let anyone near him. So I was thinking that I should examine Billy and Líadáin first, to show him that I mean no harm.' The boy's teeth and any scarring he might have would tell me about his past, I hoped.

Ms Hacker grunted softly and I took it as an agreement of some kind. Quinn entered the sitting room, slowly walking Líadáin between his legs. She was grinning widely, showing off four perfect teeth and her ability to wobble in a straight line with the help of her father.

I sank to my knees. 'You grew *so* big.' I tickled her belly. 'And chubby! You are a pumpkin, little one.'

'Best way to get my figure back,' Ms Hacker informed me. 'They suck the fat right out of me.'

Quinn coughed, then tipped his head toward the couch. 'Let's try to lure him out with cookies.'

'Has he spent the whole day there?'

'No. He hid when he saw that Billy was crying,' Quinn said.

'He's teething,' Ms Hacker supplied with a shrug.

'Hum. Let's sit, have tea and cookies, and talk. Try not to stare at him when I lure him out.'

Ms Hacker made tea, Quinn set the table, and I picked a cookie and crouched down at the back of the couch.

The boy had his face tucked against his knees, fingers of one hand splayed against the floor. As I rapped my knuckles against the floorboards, he looked up. I smiled and held out the biscuit. 'Do you remember me?'

He gave me the tiniest of nods.

'We are having tea and cookies. Do you want some?'

He flicked his gaze from my face to my outstretched hand. Hesitantly scooted forward, picked up the cookie, and nibbled at it. I moved back to give him space. After some consideration, he crept from his hiding spot.

That was quick, I thought.

He came to a halt, observing the two adults and their children. I tapped his shoulder and nodded at a chair, then walked around the table and sat down. Swallowing, he climbed on the chair and hid a hand under the table. I guessed that he was pressing his fingers against the tabletop from underneath.

The boy's gaze was bouncing between Quinn and Líadáin. He seemed puzzled by the softly amused expression in Quinn's face as little Líadáin crushed two cookies with her fists, and conveyed the crumbs to her mouth by simply dropping her face into the mess.

I tapped on the table to catch the boy's attention. Sharp hazel eyes found mine. 'I have a request if you don't mind?'

His anxious expression didn't change one bit.

'Are you a good worker?'

A small nod.

'Have you ever made preserve?'

He dropped his head, shoulders sagging.

I tapped on the table again until he looked up. 'It's all right. You are a clever boy; you can learn it.'

I scrambled to form short and clear sentences that were easy to read from my lips. 'Margery, my housekeeper, will show you. It is mostly washing fruits and vegetables, cutting them, boiling them, and filling them into clean jars. Margery has lots to do and needs help. Would you like to help?'

I had to repeat myself twice until the boy gave another small nod. But I couldn't tell if he found the prospect of jam making agreeable at all.

'We live in a house with a garden. That's where Klara picked strawberries for you. You remember Klara, my daughter, do you?'

There was a vigorous nod. A person he liked. Good.

I smiled. 'She could use a friend. If you want, you can live with us until we find your family.'

His small face lost all colour. Even his irises seemed to blanch. His body tensed, ready to curl up.

Quickly, I rapped my knuckles against the table. He peeked through his bangs.

'Do you have a mother?'

He frowned. Did he not understand the word?

'Mother,' I repeated, touching Ms Hacker's shoulder, then placed my hand on Billy's head. 'She is Billy's mother.'

The boy narrowed his eyes at little Billy who was waving his arms and legs, his face buried in Ms Hacker's bosom, making loud sucking noises as he fed.

He shook his head without looking at me.

I motioned to Líadáin on Quinn's lap, and explained that this was father and daughter, and asked the boy whether he had a father. He frowned again, seemingly undecided how to respond, and then simply shrugged.

'The man by the river, was he your father?'

The boy pressed his lips to a thin line, his eyes searching the room then dropping to the tablecloth.

'I am so sorry,' I said when he looked up again. I tried to read his face but found only confusion. 'If you could tell us where you came from, and if there is someone who is missing you, Inspector McCurley will try to find them.'

With an eerie howl, he clapped his hands to his face and dropped under the table. Quinn and I exchanged a worried look. I drew aside the tablecloth and followed the boy. He sat hunched, face tucked to his knees, fingers of one hand pressed to the rug. I began to hate this posture that screamed of terror.

I knocked, but he shook his head, refusing to look up. I knocked once more, but again he refused. So I did the only thing I could think of. Very gently, I placed my hand over his. The soft touch startled him so much, that he jumped and hit his head on the bottom of the table.

Quickly, I scooted back to give him space. He glowered at me.

'People have hurt you?'

His chin set. Eyes grew flat and cold. That wasn't an expression a six-year-old should be capable of. It was the expression of someone who had seen war. I was shocked into silence. Very slowly, I held out my hand, palm up. A gesture of peace.

He never took his eyes off mine.

'Do you know what a promise is?'

A near imperceptible nod, and still the same hard expression.

'You must know that I keep my promises. And I promise you now that you are safe with us. We will not hurt you.'

He did not move.

'I know that such a promise is hard to believe coming from a stranger. Do you still want to live in my house and help Margery make strawberry jam?'

I was sure he wanted to nod. But he pointed at Líadáin's feet that were kicking the hanging tablecloth, then pointed at himself.

'She lives here,' I said.

He pointed again at Líadáin, then at Billy, and then at himself. He curled a hand to his fist and thumped it against his chest. I wondered what it meant, then remembered Quinn telling me that the boy seemed set on protecting the babies.

'You don't want to leave the two children?'

He pushed out his lower lip and nodded once.

'I understand. I suggest a compromise. You and I come to

visit. I am a doctor. You can be my assistant. We will make sure the babies are doing well. Does that sound acceptable?'

He didn't react, just kept staring at me.

'Think about it. I will eat another cookie. Tell me what you have decided once you are ready.' I waited for a sign of agreement, then moved back onto my chair.

Grim and heartbroken silence settled in the room.

Until Quinn broke it. 'Whatever we might find out about that boy's life, it won't be pretty. And we would be ill-advised to send him back to where he came from. If we ever manage to find the place.'

5

The Boston Post, *Thursday, September 7, 1893*

MYSTIC RIVER MAN STILL UNIDENTIFIED

The body of a man found four days ago on a bank of Mystic River near Middlesex Avenue, Somerville, is still unidentified. The Somerville, Boston, and the Cambridge police departments will not say whether he was murdered or killed in an unfortunate accident. The body is laid out at the City Morgue for public viewing, and a description of the man has been publicised, but his identity remains a mystery. Every year, about a dozen of the four-hundred or so bodies brought to the City Morgue are buried without identification.

∼

I stuffed the newspaper into my briefcase, and stepped from the hansom cab onto North Grove Street. I'd never been to the Boston City Morgue, but it appeared no different from the morgues I'd seen in London:

A one-storey building tucked away in an alley with odours of death and disinfectants wafting from it. Stray cats loitered nearby, hoping to catch sight of a mortician or assistant dumping the contents of a metal bucket out of the back door.

The morgue's entrance door stood ajar. I stepped through and peeked into a corridor. A family of three — a father, mother, and a small boy — blocked my view of the receiving room. The father was shaking his head no to the boy request to prod the dead man's stomach. The parents muttered together before tugging the boy away from the gruesome sight. The family walked past me and we all nodded in greeting. The stink grew intense as I neared the rear section of the building. Two bodies were laid out in what looked like a prison cell.

A man with a soft waist, a walrus moustache, and a healthy shock of brown hair asked me if I was there to identify a body. There was a twinkle in his warm eyes that seemed at odds with the interior decoration.

I shook my head. 'Professor Goodman expects me. Dr Arlington is my name.'

'Armand Fournier,' the man said with the faintest accent and offered his hand. 'I'm the mortician. Come this way, please.'

He showed me into a small operating theatre and left. A metal table in the centre of the room was surrounded by three men, their hair and moustaches in various states of greying. The two tiers of horseshoe benches that rose behind them were populated by half a dozen young men, who smoked and chatted. Above them, sunlight dropped through an expansive skylight, cutting through swirls of dust, sweltering heat, and the thickly sweet scents of decomposition.

Anyone who'd ever caught a glimpse of a putrefying body learned the hard way that the stench is far more repulsive than the sight, that nothing punches sinuses, lungs, and mind as hard as the combined odours of excrements fermenting inside a bag of rotten meat. Nothing causes such deep revulsion, such utter alarm and an overwhelming urge to flee. And every tiny molecule of those scents is carved into memory. No one ever forgets the perfume of death.

A man in his fifties was resting a hand on the corpse's forehead and addressing the audience. 'Death due to a fall from great height may be attributed to accident, suicide, or homicide. It's difficult to differentiate the three, and especially so in this case. If you would help me move him onto his side,' he muttered to the two men next to him. They tugged on shoulder and pelvis, exposing the back of the body to the students. 'Advanced decomposition. A great number of excessive blunt force injuries. No witnesses. You can roll him back now.'

'Remains to be seen,' — one of the men in the audience bellowed — 'at the morgue.' Several others chuckled. That joke must have been decades old. I'd heard it much too often to find it amusing.

One of the students mumbled together and nodded in my direction. Silence fell. I strolled up to the metal table, scanning the corpse and the gentlemen prodding it.

'You must be Dr Arlington.' The man leading the autopsy threw a brief glance at me. Grey eyes sharpened behind spectacles. He was broad around the middle, and the top of his head was bald. His hair and beard were neatly trimmed. 'I'm Professor Goodman, the head medical examiner. You can put your things on one of the benches over there.'

Surprised, I slung off my briefcase and jacket, and rolled up my sleeves. Despite the progressiveness of the Bostonians, I kept expecting protests or at least some degree of displeasure, when taking my place beside men in an operating theatre. Professor Goodman, though, seemed to have no qualms. I suspected that my disguise was a factor. Not that I *was* disguised. Everyone could see I was a woman, just not an obviously feminine one. I wore a shirt and trousers. Stiff collar. No buffs, no frills.

From the corner of one's eye, I might have been mistaken for a male.

'Inspector McCurley told me you are a physician and a consulting detective. You don't look like you intend to be sick, so I assume he wasn't lying.' Professor Goodman winked at me.

I nearly choked at the term *consulting detective*. It brought back memories of my life back in London, and the man who'd probably coined that very term.

'The police occasionally consult me, yes, but I would describe myself as a physician only.' I walked around the table, inspecting the body that had yet to be opened. Leathery, dark brown skin was tightly stretched over bloated flesh. A lancet poked up from his abdomen, a bluish flame flickering atop it. Dirt and clothes had been removed from the body, as had most of the fly larvae.

'Solving crimes is a hobby of yours?' Goodman asked without looking up.

I smiled. Quinn had once told me that he deplored people who *played detective*. And I had *played* detective frequently. 'I have yet to ask the police for payment for my services. I guess that makes it a hobby?'

Goodman's eyebrows shot up his forehead.

I slipped my fingers along the side of the abdomen and pushed around the shoulders, ribcage, and hip. Bone fragments were shifting. I ran my hands along the neck and beneath the skull. My fingertips sunk into a soft, splintery mess. 'Is there anything left of the brain?'

'Would you like an apron?' Mr Fournier appeared at my side, holding out a fresh, white apron.

I held out my arms to him. 'Would you mind?'

Without blinking, he slipped the apron over my arms and head, and tied it at my back.

'Thank you.'

He gave me a nod.

'Most of it was eaten by maggots,' Professor Goodman said with a nod to the corpse's head. 'You were the woman who took the temperature of the first Railway Strangler victim, weren't you?'

'Hm-mm.' I wiped the gore off my fingers and crossed my hands behind my back. 'Would you mind walking me through the results of your external examination?'

'The inspector hasn't given you... Ah, of course not. We rarely give out preliminary reports. These two chaps are Drs Musgrove and Walten, by the way.' Goodman pressed his fists into his hips and stretched his back until it crackled.

Musgrove and Walten narrowed their eyes a fraction. Ah, there was the discomfiture I'd been missing.

'I must apologise for the state of this morgue,' Goodman grumbled. 'If we're lucky, the Board of Health *might* invest in a new wing. Or in regular deliveries of ice, because, *in theory*, the soapstone slab in the receiving room can be refrigerated. But there isn't even enough money to get window cleaners to scrub the pigeon droppings off the skylight. I fear any improvements will have to wait a decade. Possibly five. And they expect us to solve a murder singlehandedly in ten minutes. I wish we were as progressive as the French. Transplanting the Lyons School of Criminology to Boston would be a dream come true.'

Now *that* was a pleasant surprise. 'You follow Alexandre Lacassagne?'

'Of course, I do! Do you know him?'

'Not personally, no. I don't speak French, so I rely on translations of his works into English or German.

'Ah! I was wondering about your accent. You are German?'

'I grew up in Germany.'

'Interesting, interesting,' muttered Goodman, and threw a glance around the room. 'A little grouchy, but an excellent investigator.'

'Who?'

'Your Inspector McCurley.'

'He is not my...' I shook my head.

Professor Goodman coughed. 'Now, you must know that not everyone agrees with me on the superiority of Lacassagne's research. Dr Walten here, still believes Lombroso's theories have value, for example. The fool — Lombroso, that is — just published a study you might find as repulsive as I. It is titled "The Female Offender," and describes the impulses ruling the minds of women criminals. And prostitutes as well. He sees women as underdeveloped and unevolved — primitive version of men.'

I snorted.

'It amuses you? Well, I guess humour is sorely needed when scientists aim their ridiculous opinions at you.'

I shrugged, hiding the anger that roiled in my stomach. 'A *scientist* whose only goal is to prove his own hypotheses, but never tries to disprove them, is not a scientist. He might rather be compared to a showman or even a clergyman. That buffoon Lombroso is not alone in his beliefs and outdated methods. Many anthropologists, Darwin included, believe that women are less evolved than men. And so they measured hundreds upon hundreds of skulls to show that, on average, the skulls of women are smaller than those of men. But none of those *scientists* actually measured intelligence. None of them was able to find a shred of evidence for a correlation between intraspecific variations in brain size and intellect.' I could have gone on and on. But long-winded, angry speeches rarely had the effect of making people see my point.

Goodman used his wrist to push his spectacles up his nose, then looked sharply at his students. 'And that, dear chaps, is why we would do well to welcome more women into our midst.'

I was as stunned as everyone else in the room. Faces fell. Diplomacy didn't seem to be Goodman's forte. I was liking him very much already.

Again, he winked at me. 'Now, you asked for the results of the external examination. Nothing unusual or surprising there. Open fractures of the skull, spine, and pelvis. Hematoma and abrasions along the length of the trunk. All the injuries are confined to a single surface plane of the body — the back to be precise — on which he fell. Faint post-mortem lividity is present on his left side. He bled out pretty fast. No hesitation marks or grab marks. Several small tears in his shirt and vest.'

I nodded. Hesitation marks, such as scarring of the wrists, would have pointed to a history of suicide attempts. Grab marks would indicate that the man had been dragged to a bridge, a balcony or the like, and pushed off. 'Are the tears in his clothes from transporting the body, or from the impact?'

'Most likely from grabbing and transporting it. Please light the flue for us now, Dr Musgrove.' At that, Professor Goodman clapped his gory hands and announced the autopsy would begin.

Musgrove held a match to a large, funnel-shaped box below the table upon which the corpse lay. There was a hiss of gas. Puzzled, I cocked my head at him.

'The flame produces a downward draught through the perforated table, carrying off most of the disagreeable odours,' Dr Musgrove explained.

'*In theory*,' added Professor Goodman, and signalled to Dr

Walten, who picked up a knife and sliced the body open from chin to pubic bone. The stench was unbearable. Sweet, thick, heavy. Coating everything from my clothes to my eyeballs. Or so it felt.

The urge to vomit tickled my tongue. That reflex had always been there and would always stay with me. I'd learned to control it when I witnessed my first postmortem more than a decade earlier. Forcing the back of my mouth and throat to relax, I blinked once and focused on the matter at hand.

The list of internal injuries was long. Ruptures of several of the large blood vessels. Cardiac, bronchus, liver, and spleen ruptures. Fractures of the ribs, pelvis, shoulders, neck, and skull. The impact had shredded the brain, killing the man instantly.

Dr Walten bottled samples of the maggot and brain tissue mixture, and of the decomposed remains of heart, liver, and stomach contents for the toxicologist.

'We took samples of the fauna when the body arrived at the morgue,' Goodman told me several hours later after we had shed our aprons and scrubbed the gore off our hands and forearms. 'The microscopist has identified each of the species and their developmental stages, and is now comparing these to the most recent study of the Parisian entomologist Jean Pierre Mégnin. I'm in regular communication with him. With Monsieur Mégnin, that is. He is developing a timetable, a study which he calls "Fauna of Tombs," which describes the succession of arthropods colonising corpses. Beetles, mites, flies, and so on. Extraordinarily interesting! I have each of his letters translated, and make copies for my students.' He looked from me to the small crowd of men. 'Colmer!' he barked. 'Give your copy to Dr Arlington.'

I cringed at Goodman's lack of finesse. 'I couldn't possibly accept—'

'Hurry up, Colmer. You're never going to read it anyway.'

With a fiery red face, the young man fumbled with his notes, extracted a narrow folder, and brought it over to me.

'Thank you. I'll return it—'

'Never mind.' Colmer looked past me to shoot a glare at Goodman.

'Now,' the professor continued undisturbed, 'Monsieur Mégnin is finding that the succession of insect species and their developmental states is highly predictable and can aid in pinpointing time of death.'

I glanced down at the notes in my hand. One sentence struck me at once. *The workers of death only arrive at their table successively and always in the same order.*

'Fascinating,' I breathed, and received a pointy elbow to my side.

'It is, isn't it?' Goodman grunted good-naturedly, and told his assistants to peel all the flesh off the bones by the following morning, and, while doing so, to repeat the examination of every square inch of skin for marks that might help identify the corpse. 'Your Inspector has an inkling. So we are checking twice. Drs Musgrove and Walten will once again catalogue each scar, and add any old fracture to the list.'

'What about dental work?'

He shook his head. 'Nothing. He had unusually healthy teeth for a man of his age. No cavities or missing teeth, no signs of rickets or congenital syphilis. No stains that would indicate heavy smoking, and no wear marks from the stem of a pipe.'

I LEFT the confines of North Grove Street and its morgue, tipped my face at the afternoon sky and let the cool breeze dry my sweaty temples. Dr Walten's farewell was a dull echo in the back of my head. When Professor Goodman was out of earshot, Walten had bent close to me and hissed, 'How do you justify taking the post of a qualified man?'

I'd smiled at him. Not too long ago, that same question would have been yelled at me in front of my peers had anyone known I was masquerading as a male physician. Now, though, men like Walten had to mutter their beliefs behind shut doors. Men like Walten were outdated. Dinosaurs. And in a decade or two, they'd be mere side notes of history, the ridicule of the human species.

Yes, sometimes I wallowed in naive hope.

I filled my lungs with fresh air and imagined the stink of decomposing corpse sluicing off my bronchi like a layer of rancid fat off a skillet. Longing for a hot bath and fresh clothes, I hailed a cab.

When I reached home and stepped out of the hansom, I saw Zachary rip open the door to the house, his gaze and jaw hard. I knew then that comfort would have to wait. All the hairs on my neck rose in alarm. 'What happened?'

'He's gone.'

'Who?'

'The boy. The deaf boy is gone.'

6

'One minute, the children were playing, and the next, Klara was crying and the boy gone.' Zach spoke over his shoulder as we walked into the kitchen.

Klara sat at the table, her nose deep in a cup. She had a small scratch on her cheek. A milk moustache stretched wide as she looked up and smiled at me.

'Do you know where he went?' I asked her.

She licked the milk off her upper lip and shook her head. Her dark thistledown hair sported small fragments of twigs, leaves, and grass.

I turned to Zach. 'Show me where you looked for him, and where he was before he disappeared.'

We searched the garden, the house and annex, and the neighbourhood. I learned from Zach that the children had been climbing trees and playing hide-and-seek. When they started fencing with sticks, things got a bit rough, and the boy smacked Klara on the cheek. As soon as she started crying, he ran.

'He thinks we'll punish him.'

Zach mumbled agreement. The sun was beginning to set

and I wondered whether we should send a note to Quinn. There was a possibility the boy had run all the way to his house.

We found Klara in the garden, searching for her playmate. Before Zach went back into the house, I stopped him. 'Tell Margery to set the table on the porch. He might come out when he sees that we are having dinner.'

BUT HE DIDN'T SHOW up. Not a peep, not a rustle from him. My worry grew. Klara picked her plate clean and was soon staring at our apple and cherry trees, hoping, perhaps, the boy would drop from them like an overripe fruit.

My thoughts drifted back to my visit to Quinn's the previous afternoon when I examined the two babies. The girl's hip had made progress; her dysplasia was barely even detectable. But when I'd asked the boy whether I could examine him as well, he'd bristled. He had only agreed to it when I placed Ms Hacker's son on my lap and allowed the boy to sit next to us on the floor and hold the baby's hand. A brief examination, superficial as it was, told me that — aside from malnourishment and various skin infections — he seemed comparatively healthy. Unsurprisingly, he'd had no dental work done that would help identify him.

Later that evening, Margery had stuck him into our bathtub and combed out an unfathomable quantity of lice, ignoring his protests and yet somehow managing to not scare him off.

Klara tore me from my thoughts. She reached out a hand and patted mine. And that's when I heard it.

A small cough.

My gaze snapped to the toolshed. We'd searched it earlier. And even the old privy next to it.

I held up my hand to silence the others, and waited for

another noise. None came. Zach and I rose and walked toward the shed. I wished the songbirds would cease their blaring for a moment or two, so I could hear…

There was a soft whimper. It was unmistakable.

'Where did it come from?' I whispered.

Zach pointed to the privy. I frowned. Wouldn't someone have noticed if the boy had crossed the garden and sneaked into the privy?

I opened the door and saw…nothing.

Zach stepped around me and moved the lid of the privy seat aside. I pushed the door open farther to let more light in.

'There you are.' Zach stuck his arms into the privy and lifted a dishevelled and terrified scrap of a boy out. 'You're lucky no one's used this thing for years.'

'I thought it was all filled up with soil?'

'Still enough space for a small boy to squeeze in, it seems.' The child clung to Zach like a barnacle, his face tucked firmly against the grown man's throat.

Unspeaking, we returned to the table. Klara spread butter on a slice of bread and plopped it on the boy's plate. Margery cut thick slices of salami and pushed them over to him. He stuffed the food into his mouth with dirty fingers, streaks of old tears smudging his face. After the third sandwich was devoured, I tapped my knuckles on the table. 'Do you want to tell me what happened?'

He made a tentative gesture at Klara's cheek.

'Did you apologise to her?'

His chin trembled and his gaze was darting around the table. Zach made an effort to appear busy with a smattering of breadcrumbs on the tablecloth, and Margery meticulously arranged her butter knife parallel to her plate.

Abruptly, the boy grasped Klara's hand and shook it.

'It's all right. It doesn't hurt anymore,' she squeaked.

I nearly choked on my own spittle. Up until that day, the

rare one-word sentence was all she'd ever said. Zach and Margery were frozen in mid-movement. I scrambled to find words.

Klara poked a finger at the boy. 'We *said* no hiding in the privy. It's gross! People *pooped* in it.'

My cheeks were aching. A chuckle burst from my mouth, and within a heartbeat, we were holding our bellies with laughter.

'Well, I'm glad no one's pooped in it for a decade or so.' Zach wiped his eyes. 'And you, young man, will take a bath now.'

LATER, Klara read to the boy, whose gaze bounced between her mouth and the letters on the page. Suddenly, she stopped and asked his name.

He clenched his jaw and shook his head.

'But I *want* to know!'

His eyes narrowed as he thrust his chin toward the book in her lap. He tapped the pages, demanding that she keep reading.

'Mama?'

'I wish you could tell us your name,' I said to the boy.

He shook his head, flopping his wet hair. Margery had made him bathe twice that day. She'd combed his head for lice, and made sure his infected skin was covered from head to toe with an unguent I'd prepared.

I hated that we kept calling him *the boy*. Grasping at straws, I said the first thing that came to my mind, 'You could pick a name for the time being. Like the heroes of old. They got to pick their own names, too.'

He squinted at my mouth. His expression brightened a little.

'You don't need to know your letters. Just point at

pictures,' I continued as goose bumps flitted over my skin. 'Björn is the bear. Arne is the eagle and Eikar the oak. Take your time and choose well. A name has power.'

～

ZACH HAD MANAGED to fix my bicycle, so I was again enjoying the freedom it offered. After spending part of the morning at Ward Six, I rode to the morgue to inquire about results of the examination of the bones. The mortician informed me that none of the medical examiners was present and that a preliminary report had been sent to the detective investigating the case. Mr Fournier pinched his walrus moustache. 'But if you wish to speak to the microscopist, you'll find him in the laboratory.'

'I love microscopes!' I blurted.

Mr Fournier puffed up his cheeks and showed the way.

The microscopist was a hovering over his instrument like a heron over a frog. A small, bright electrical lamp served as the only light source, casting long shadows into the gloom. He merely grunted when we entered the small room. His eyes and left hand kept going to and fro between the microscope and a notebook.

'It might take a while,' Fournier whispered in my ear, and left.

I watched as drawing after drawing blossomed on the pages of his notebook, his short hair growing more and more disorderly with each absentminded scratching of pencil against scalp. On his workbench lay a flat white stone. A small shape was drawn on it. Intrigued, I picked it up. No, nothing had been drawn on it. It had been fashioned. 'A caddisfly larva,' I muttered.

The chair screeched on the floor, as the man jerked back.

'Godalmighty, you gave me a heart attack.' Rubbing his chest, he glared at me.

'My apologies. Dr Elizabeth Arlington is my name. I'm assisting Inspector McCurley. Are you looking at samples from the Mystic River man?'

'Who is that Inspector...' He twirled a hand in the air. '...McCurley?'

'The detective leading the case.'

'Oh.' He picked up his notebook, held it close to his face and leafed through the pages. 'Ah. Yes. Inspector Quinn McCurley. Leading Detective. Short. Blue eyes. Moustache. Prominent scar on right side of face. Grumpy.' When he looked back up, I noticed that the eyepieces of his microscope had left imprints around his eyes. I swallowed a laugh.

'My brain has no room for names. What was yours again? Mine is Allston. Actually, *Dr* Allston, but the PhD certificate looks like someone smeared ink on toilet paper. So Allston will suffice.' He wiped his hand on his trousers and thrust it out to me.

'Elizabeth Arlington. Pleased to meet you.'

'Are you? Strange. What was it that you wanted? I'm rather busy.' He moved both hands back to the microscope, half turning away, ready to dismiss me.

I pinched my lips together to hide a grin. 'I used to own a Zeiss a few years back. The stacked lenses produced a clarity and sharpness I've yet to see elsewhere.'

He blinked at me. Then at his microscope. With a small cough, he offered me his chair. I sat down and looked through the two eyepieces. 'Lung tissue. HE stained?'

'Yes.'

'It's beautiful. I've always thought of it as an art. Preparing and staining tissues and cells for microscopy, I mean.' He did not reply, and I took my time scanning the lung tissue sections shining brilliantly in shades of red and blue. 'Looks healthy. What about the liver? Were glycogen and glucose present?

'Of course.' His clothes rustled as he shifted and leant back against the wall behind him.

'The man died on the spot. Had a pretty big hole in his head, after all.' I pushed back from the microscope and looked at Dr Allston. 'You catalogued the insect developmental stages, I heard. Did you find anything interesting?'

Here, he lit up. Even his disorderly hair seemed to stand up with glee. 'This time of year, the eggs of houseflies and blowflies are deposited in open wounds and soft parts like mouth and eyes within minutes. Then come the *Sacrophaga* — flesh flies. Excellent parents, all of them, if you ask me. Better than *some humans*. Flies secure optimum conditions and sufficient nutrition for their offspring for far longer than they need for their development. Certain beetle and moth species are still happy to gnaw on the fibrous leftovers months later. Er... What was your question again?'

'If you found anything—'

'Ah, yes, I remember now. I found the usual suspects. Nothing that would help pinpoint where he died or where his body was kept until someone dumped it by the river. But!' He held up a finger, then pointed it to the flat white pebble I'd held in my hand earlier. 'There were several of those in his pockets. For whatever reasons. He must have picked them up by the river because on three of the stones I found partial tubes of caddisfly larvae. *Polycentropodidae* to be precise.'

I brushed my finger over the pebble in his hand. 'He was skipping stones.'

'Skipping stones? Why would anyone do that?'

THE OFFICER at the receiving desk informed me that

Inspector McCurley was not available. I left him a message, asking for a meeting at my home when convenient.

Margery was pickling cucumbers when I returned. The boy cut onions and Klara ground mustard seeds in a mortar. She was giggling when I entered the kitchen. 'Arthur makes the onions naked!'

Margery groaned and rolled her eyes heavenward. 'God's nightgown.'

It seemed as if, once Klara started speaking in whole sentences, the floodgates stood open. She placed the pestle aside and ran loops around the kitchen table, singing 'Arthur makes the onions go naked!' Every time she passed by him, she slapped him on the bum. He was grinning.

'You chose a good name,' I said when he caught my gaze.

He pointed at Klara.

'She picked your name?'

A nod and a smile.

'You want to keep it?'

The smile broadened.

'King Arthur.' I produced a bow. 'I brought you something. But please, finish disrobing the onions first.'

He squinted at my mouth. Perhaps he didn't know the word *disrobing*.

'Make the onions naked, Arthur,' I added with a grin.

Klara ran another couple of rounds, squeaking her song, and Margery huffed yet another 'God's nightgown' toward the ceiling.

A LITTLE WHILE LATER, Arthur and I sat on the steps of the porch. I pulled the white stone from my pocket and held it in my palm for him to see. He gulped and produced a shocked hiccup.

'You know this?'

He nodded.

I made a sweeping gesture with my arm. 'Did he make the stones dance over the water?'

Another small nod.

'You liked him, didn't you?'

His nostrils flared. Silver was pooling in his eyes. Sniffing, he looked out into the garden. I waited, listening to the birds, saddened that he'd never hear them.

Finally, he gave me a nod.

'Inspector McCurley and I are trying to find out what happened to him. Can you help us?'

His gaze darted away. Again, I waited until his chin dipped. I touched my elbow to his side. 'Thank you. I will ask you a few questions. Let me know when you don't understand or if you want to take a break.'

He seemed to age in a heartbeat.

'Did he tell you his name?'

He opened his mouth and formed a word that I couldn't make out. Why did no one deem it necessary to teach him sign language?

'Another question, then. Did you see how he died?'

A nod. And a dark flicker in his eyes.

'Did he jump?'

He shook his head no.

'Fall?'

A pause. Again he shook his head. He lifted both hands, index and middle fingers pointed down, miming two persons running. One followed by the other. Climbing steps of a stair or a ladder. Bumping into one another. One falling. One staying behind.

He dropped his hands in his lap and curled them to fists. I reached out, but he scooted away from me. This was so hard. So many questions and so few ways to ask and answer them.

Sighing, I knelt in front of him and told him that I was

sorry. I asked if he'd like to tell me more, or if he'd rather ask Klara to read a chapter of King Author's story to him. He put his palms together, then slowly opened them. *I want to read.*

I FOUND Margery in the kitchen and asked if anyone had answered the job advertisement I'd put in the papers the previous day.

'Two men called. Zachary didn't like them. And then there was a governess who insisted on living here. I didn't like *her.*'

'Hum. If we can't find a tutor, we have to send the boy back to the school for deaf children. And I doubt that's a good idea. One of the teachers brought him to the police stations for…well, crying.'

'Any muffins left?' Zach rumbled through the door. Margery pointed him to the bread basket. 'Don't worry, Liz,' he mumbled through his full mouth. 'They'll come. It's still more than an hour to dinner time.'

A dishtowel smacked against Zach's behind. 'You always think in mealtimes!' Margery hissed.

He grinned. 'Because I'm married to someone who—'

The bell rang.

'…wields magic in the kitchen,' Zach muttered after Margery, who had already left the kitchen to get the door.

'That'll be the next applicant for the tutor job,' he said, at the same moment I said, 'That'll be Inspector McCurley.'

But instead, a tall, handsome man stepped into the kitchen.

7

*H*is wavy black hair was longer than the last time I'd seen him. The set of his shoulders was stiff, as was his gait. He looked a bit frayed around the edges, and I wondered if he was still suffering repercussions from the stunt he'd pulled three months before.

'Warren, it's…good to see you.' I was too surprised by his unexpected visit to know what to say.

He raised an eyebrow. 'It's been a long time.'

'Yes, it has. Shall we go to the—'

'Sitting room. I'll bring tea,' Margery interrupted. I shot her an irritated glance. She'd been in a strangely pushy mood since Arthur had moved in with us.

I motioned for Warren to go ahead. Too tall for the doorway, he had to stoop a little as he entered the sitting room. He found an armchair and folded himself onto it, then scanned my face. 'You never came. Not once. Why?'

I perched on the armrest of the couch, regarding him quizzically. 'Whatever do you mean?'

'The Freaks' nights. Was it…' Frowning, he drew a thumb across his brow. 'Was it so easy to forget us?'

'You thought I would go back to normal in a matter of days?'

He shrugged. Then shook his head. An undecided gesture. He hadn't thought it all through, what he would say to me that first time when we first met again.

'How is everyone?' I asked.

He stood and walked over to the bay window, drew the curtain aside and propped a foot on the low sill, his back to me. 'Well... Uriel's wife has filed for divorce. Naturally, Jerome is getting his hopes up. Doesn't help to tell him Uriel is not into buggery. Hattie is about to pop, but you know that. And Father threw me out of my townhouse and cut my allowance to a fraction of what it was. It's a pittance, really.' Over his shoulder, he levelled a stare at me. 'It's all been quite the catastrophe.'

I grew cold. 'You came here to blame me?'

He reared back, his shoulder nearly colliding with the window pane. 'Of course not. I blame myself. After all, I was the one who drew your portraits and lost them. My fault the Railway Strangler got his hands on them. You nearly died, for Christ's sake! You had to go through all this, and I...and I *lied* to you. I'm a bastard.' He turned away once more and stared out into the garden. After a long beat of silence, he swivelled his pale blue gaze back at me. 'Are you well?'

'I am. Thank you. But how about you?'

He groaned. 'Enough of the small talk already. Come back to us. The Freaks miss you. *I* miss you.'

I dropped my eyes to the rug. 'I don't think it's a good idea. Uriel's wife blames me for what happened.'

'I hate to say it, but... She's planning to take you to court for libel and manslaughter.'

My heart leapt into my throat. 'Is she mad?'

'Probably. She still believes that you and Uriel were having an affair, that you somehow manipulated the Railway

Strangler case so that her brother would be implicated, and then you made sure he would come to your house so Inspector McCurley could shoot him dead.'

My brain felt hollow. 'W-what?'

'She believes the evidence against her brother was fabricated. By you.'

'Does it run in the family? The madness? Her brother blamed me for breaking his nose years ago. Can you imagine that? I never even *met* the man before he tried to strangle me.' That last bit was not entirely true. I probably had met him briefly at Harvard Medical School, and then forgot his name and face. I'd been masquerading as a man back then, and had never expected any of my old colleagues to recognise me.

But Warren didn't need to know any of that. It was far too complicated and dangerous to explain. 'He hated me for simply existing! I can't even... I don't understand why he killed those women. Why he tried to kill me. He seemed... unstable. Out of his mind. If it's true what you're saying, his sister seems to be cultivating the same trait.'

'Unfortunately, it's true.' Warren slumped back into his chair, stretched out his long legs, put his head in his neck, and shut his eyes. 'You know, we...the Freaks, we... We nearly fell apart after that. Haywood destroyed a marriage, tested friendships. If he weren't dead, I would punch his balls bloody.' He opened his eyes. 'Come back to us, Liz. It's only Uriel's stupid wife who blames you. Everyone else blames me. Rightfully so.'

'You didn't kill anyone, Warren. And...I'm not sure I'm ready. It's been a hard time. But I promise you, I will join you again soon.'

He frowned. 'I can hear another *but* coming.

I dipped my head. 'I'm pretty busy right now. We've taken in a young boy, and I'm investigating a...crime.' History was repeating itself. I couldn't help but grin.

'*Again?* Wasn't the last attempt horrible enough?'

I was taken aback. 'What do you mean by *attempt?* I led the Railway Stranger into a trap. If he hadn't tried so hard to kill me and escape, he would have been arrested, not shot dead. And what *precisely* are you trying to tell me anyway?'

'I'm trying to tell you to take better care of yourself.'

'Your chivalry is misplaced.'

His shoulders sagged, and he began worrying his lower lip with his teeth. 'I came here to apologise for lying to you, and for pretending...' He motioned at his face. 'For pretending to be shot. For pretending the Railway Strangler did it. And I w-w-wanted to let you kn-n-ow that I meant what I said when I kissed you.'

Admitting this was costing Warren. The stutter he'd been fighting since childhood was peeking through. I was about to reply when the doorbell rang. *Again.* I flicked my gaze toward the corridor, listening for Margery to clonk the kettle against the range and stomp to the door.

Warren must have sensed that I didn't quite know what to say to him, so he swiftly changed the topic. 'Oh, and my dear twin sister told me to remind you that your telephone will be installed tomorrow morning at eight.'

I groaned. 'I completely forgot about that!' I didn't look forward to a telephone in the house. The thing was loud and would probably ring at least twice a week. But Hattie was worried. She'd be having twins and her biggest nightmare was that her labour would be short and intense, and her babies would shoot out into the night before I even made it to her home. Or worse, they'd get stuck and die. And so she insisted that the telephone company connect our house. And she'd insisted on paying for it.

Voices trickled down the corridor. That of a young woman and...Quinn? I stood when Margery arrived with two guests. A girl I didn't know was followed closely by

Quinn, who carried his daughter in his arms. Líadáin — decked out in white frills — was sucking at her fist, her eyes wide and bright.

The young woman looked at Quinn and he back at her, each waiting for the other to speak first.

'Did you come for the tutor post?' I asked.

She bounced on her heels. 'Yes, I did! I wanted to come earlier this morning, but Father wouldn't permit it.' She clapped a hand to her mouth. 'I mean…at *first,* he didn't, but then he agreed. I know sign language, numbers, letters, and cooking. Annie Lowell is my name.'

Margery eyed her warily.

'I should be leaving.' Warren stood and frowned at Líadáin in Quinn's arms. I could only guess what was going through his mind.

Quinn stilled. The two men measured one another for a cold moment. They had a brief and unpleasant history. To escape an arranged marriage, Warren had pretended he'd been shot in the face by the Railway Strangler. It was Quinn who'd instantly seen through the charade. Warren's influential father pulled a few strings so that only a fine had to be paid, rather than a prison sentence served for obstructing an ongoing police investigation. And after all was said and done, Warren's father had cut his son's access to the enormous family purse.

There was no love lost between Warren and Quinn.

I cleared my throat. 'I'll probably telephone you,' I said to Warren, and to the girl, 'The children are reading in the garden. I want you to meet them.'

'Should I return tomorrow?' Quinn asked.

'No. This won't take long. Would you like to stay for dinner?'

'I don't want to inconvenience you.'

'Nonsense,' Margery said from behind him as she showed a somewhat perplexed Warren to the door.

I INTRODUCED Miss Lowell to Klara and Arthur, then retreated to the porch to watch from a distance. Margery had placed cups, tea, milk, and sliced apples on the table. Líadáin slobbered on a piece of fruit, but wouldn't be confined to Quinn's lap. He carried her down the steps and set her on the grass.

'I hope you don't mind me bringing her. Billy and Miss Hacker had a rough night, and they were sleeping when I left.'

'Bring her any time you like. Miss Hacker and Billy are welcome, too.' I supposed she didn't get out much. Young mothers from the lower classes rarely ventured far from than the block they lived on. Many saw no point experiencing more than just the four walls of their home, and the shops and hawkers in the neighbourhood.

'I try not to encourage her,' Quinn replied.

'You think she still fancies you?'

He looked up and tilted his head. 'Is that so unlikely?'

I opened my mouth and clicked it shut. At first, I didn't understand what he was getting at, but slowly it dawned on me. He thought the scar on the side of his face made him look repulsive.

'Yes,' I said truthfully.

His expression emptied.

'I haven't sensed anything like that from her. But I could never quite relate to the rules of attraction, so I'm not the best person to ask. But I can imagine that she...' *Damn, I should have just kept my mouth shut.*

'Feels obliged?'

'No, I'm pretty sure Miss Hacker doesn't function that

way. If, as you say, she wants more from you than just employment, it's because of what she observes. She sees that you are a loving father to Líadáin, and concludes that her son would find a good father in you, and she a good husband.'

His ears reddened as a smile flitted across his face. 'You treat everything like a scientific experiment.'

Prickling ran up my arms. I shifted my gaze away from his. 'Have you had any luck with your investigation?'

He produced a soft grunt, and told me about the orphanages, almshouses, and children's asylums he and Boyle had telephoned and visited. Several dozen children of Arthur's age were missing, but no one seemed bothered by it. The children were unruly, disliked school, and tolerated the switch for a few days of freedom.

'They might eventually be reported missing if no one has seen them for a week or two,' he said. 'Or they won't be reported at all, and their cot will be given to another child. For our boy, though, this is all irrelevant because there are no deaf children missing. But I was thinking… Would you mind taking the boy with you next time you go to Wards Six and Seven? Someone there might recognise him.'

'I'm reluctant to expose him to anything that'll remind him of his past. I know it's counterproductive. But it's just that—'

'You want to protect him.'

'Yes. But I know I can't. We need to know what happened. Klara gave him a name today. Arthur. From the legend.'

'*King* Arthur?'

'Yes.'

'Is she supposed to be eating that?' Quinn dashed toward his daughter who was conveying a wriggling earthworm to her mouth. She cried when he pried it from her grasp.

I broke out laughing. 'I knew she'd be completely engrossed with the garden. Klara tasted worms, beetles, spiders, and whatever flower she could find. I made sure there are no poisonous plants growing here. So of course she went after a hornet. I nearly got cardiac arrest.'

Startled, he could only blink. 'I've seen my share of blood and guts, but watching my child get hurt is a brand new level of pain.'

'Paternal instincts are terrifying.'

'They are. Which brings me back to the boy. We are trying to keep him out of the newspapers. So if anyone comes asking, you don't know anything.' He brushed soil and bits of grass off his daughter's face, and turned, his expression darkening. 'The preliminary report stated that three faint scratches were found at the back of the corpse's head. They would match the fingernails of a small hand. The scratches were only visible after they cut the hair away from the head wound and reconstructed the flaps of skin. It's quite possible that the boy scratched him at some point. He might have been holding Arthur in his arms just before he died. The boy saw something. I'm quite sure.'

'He saw the man was pushed.' I told Quinn what Arthur had conveyed to me with his hand signals — the chase and then the fall of one man as the other watched. Silence fell as we spotted Annie Lowell leaving Klara and Arthur by the old apple tree where they sat reading a book. Had she known what Quinn and I were talking about, she wouldn't have looked so cheerful.

The evening sun bounced off her ruddy cheeks and chestnut hair as she clapped her hands reaching us. 'The children are adorable! But I must have misread the advertisement. Someone has already taught Arthur sign language.'

'Are you saying that he *knows* sign language?' I was baffled.

She bobbed her head. 'He signed "thank you" and "friend."

But I don't know how much he understood of what I signed to him. He is very timid.'

'Odd. A teacher from the school for deaf children said Arthur doesn't know sign language at all.'

'Ah.' She picked at her sleeves and said no more.

Quinn opened his mouth, but I shook my head at him. 'Our tea is getting cold. Join us for a moment, Miss Lowell.'

*a*nnie Lowell promised to return the following day. Humming a ditty, she clanked the garden gate shut and marched up along Savin Hill Avenue.

Líadáin was sitting on Quinn's lap, soaking saliva into a muffin. A corner of his mouth curled. 'You offered a tutor post to a filly.'

I grinned. 'Yes. She's exactly what I was looking for. Kind-hearted, funny, and a most unlikely person to discipline the children.'

He frowned at that. 'An unusual approach.'

I pushed a slice of apple into Líadáin's grasping hand. 'You disapprove? Would you use the switch on *her*? Wasn't it you who said that watching your own child get hurt is a brand new level of pain?'

His posture stiffed as his expression went from thoughtful to angry to decisive. 'I know what violence does to a man. I will not do that to my child.' His gaze slid from his daughter to Klara and Arthur, who'd given up reading and were rolling sideways down the gentle slope of the garden. 'Or any child, actually.'

I felt his eyes on me then. Unsure what to do with my hands or my face, I took a sip of tea.

'Is that a weakness?' he asked softly. 'You know more about parenting than I. Isn't a father supposed to discipline his children?'

I set my cup into my lap and stared down at it. 'You once told me that you used to be a pit fighter. Would you consider it honourable for a man to beat up another half his size?'

'Of course not!'

'There's your answer. If you ask me for parenting advice I can only tell you this: don't listen to parenting advice.'

He guffawed. Líadáin's spit out her mushed apple, threw back her head, and laughed at her father.

'Listen to your heart. You love your daughter, and she loves and trusts you. No matter how brilliant a father you are, you can be assured that she'll do stupid and reckless things that'll make your heart stop.'

'If that ain't the truth. Klara! You and Arthur, go wash your hands and face. Dinner's on the table in ten minutes!' Margery hollered through the kitchen window.

Quinn sat up straighter. 'We keep getting distracted.'

'We are horrible detectives. Tell me more about the preliminary report.'

He did. There was nothing I didn't already know, but we needed to summarise the findings and go through them, poking for holes, and finding many new questions among the few answers we had: The man had fallen from a great height and died on impact. Arthur had seen a struggle and possibly a chase of the dead man by another person. The scratches on the back of the man's head could have been caused by Arthur. I'd ask him about it. It was established that Arthur and the man had known one another, and were possibly friends. But a lot remained unclear.

'It keeps bothering me,' Quinn said, combing his fingers

through Líadáin's hair. 'Why hide the body for a week in the summer heat, and then move it? And why dump it by the river when the tide had just gone out? Why leave perfect footprints and a body in plain sight?'

'Haste? Panic? You can't expect them to plan and think like you.'

'Hum. Let's assume for a moment that they planned for the body to be taken away by the tide. They checked the tide schedule for Boston harbour. And then they missed it by an hour or more? It makes no sense. But then...people who kill in a passion, who don't plan or even think straight, are the ones we catch. The murderers who calmly plot a killing — those are the ones we never find. The question remains — was this killing done on the spur of the moment, or was it an impulse or an accident? The evidence suggests it wasn't planned. To me, this looks like the perpetrators panicked and couldn't decide what do with the body. I don't think they planned any of this.'

'Can you tell from stride length and boot size and depth of the footprints that they were men?' I asked

He shook his head. 'No, not with any certainty. Not all women are dainty little things, and not all men are big brutes.'

'I always like to disprove hypotheses. So let's assume they planned everything. Meticulously. They planned the killing, and they planned how to get rid of the body. But then... something happened. Something unforeseen.' I scratched my head. 'Along the way, they made a mistake. Reading tide tables is simple, I doubt they misread them.'

I felt Quinn's piercing gaze on me. The tiny hairs on my arms rose in answer.

He said, 'Did they misread them or were they held up on the way?' He trailed off, his eyes narrowing. Líadáin slammed both hands flat on the table and sent the plate in front of her flying. With a deft flick of his hand, Quinn caught it.

'The skipping stones,' I murmured as he stood and began rocking his wriggly daughter. 'She's probably hungry. I'll ask Margery to bring porridge.'

'No, she's tired and wants Miss Hacker. I'll take my leave. We can continue our discussion tomorrow.'

'If it's all right with you, I can feed her. Klara weaned herself when Arthur arrived because she doesn't want him to think she's a baby. So I have a...um...surplus of milk at the moment.'

Quinn stopped in his tracks. Líadáin began to cry. 'You would...her...' He'd got stuck on the work "breastfeed."

Feigning indifference, I produced a shrug. 'I'm a mammal, she's a mammal.'

Blood rose to his ears, but he took a step closer and handed me his daughter. As he sat back down and made a point of looking out onto the garden, I unbuttoned my shirt and offered Líadáin a breast. I hoped this would calm her down enough to fall asleep. 'It might be as simple as a broken watch,' I ventured.

Quinn huffed. 'It might be as simple as that. It was still dark when they got rid of the body. They might not have seen that the tide wasn't coming in, but going out already.'

'Nor have they seen that they were leaving footprints. But they must have felt their boots sinking into the mud.'

'The skipping stones.' His gaze strayed to me and quickly averted again. Women breastfeeding in public was a common enough sight, but for some reason my doing it was making Quinn uncomfortable. He'd had no such qualms with Miss Hacker nursing his daughter and her own son in their sitting room.

He cleared his throat. 'They were skipping stones by the

sea or the river. I wish we could limit that to a single location.'

'We can limit it somewhat. Caddisfly larvae need fresh water.'

'A river or lake, then. Good. Next, we need to know where Arthur comes from and if that's where he met the man and witnessed his death. Will you ask the boy?'

'I can't guarantee an answer,' I said softly so as not to disturb Líadáin. Her small fist kneading my shirt grew slack and settled against my breastbone. Her eyes fluttered shut. 'There you go, dear one.'

The *clomp-clomp* of Margery's shoes made Líadáin twitch. Luckily, it didn't wake her. 'Would you like to take dinner here, or later in the sitting room?' she asked.

'Can you bring it out, please?'

She paused for a moment as she spotted Líadáin attached to my breast. Only as she left did I notice that Quinn was eerily quiet. I scanned his profile. A muscle in his jaw rippled. 'I'm sorry,' I said softly.

He didn't look at me. 'What are you sorry for?' His voice was gruff.

'This makes you sad. It reminds you of your wife.' Nine months earlier, Quinn's wife had leapt from their third-floor window, planning to take their daughter down with her. Quinn had managed to save Líadáin, but only barely.

'Don't apologise. Líadáin reminds me of Ailis every day. It's just that...' He shook his head once. I waited. Behind us in the house, Zachary and Margery talked about Mr and Mrs Cratchitt's brood of many children, and what kind of cake to bake for Klara's birthday.

'You are still worried about her third birthday,' Quinn said, his eyes narrowed to a spot on my thigh where I hid my holster. 'You had a tailor conceal an opening in your clothing so you can reach your revolver at any times?'

I nodded. 'Zach carries one as well. There's always at least one armed person around Klara.'

'You are a study in contrasts,' he murmured, and then with insistence, 'When does she turn three?'

'In a week.'

'I'll be here. Will you be safe after that?'

I shook my head.

'Explain it to me.'

I pulled my shirt closed, and softly rocked Líadáin as I collected my thoughts. 'Moran, the man who threatened to take her from me when she turns three, is in Europe. He's under surveillance and I receive weekly wires on his location. The detective following him has identified nearly of all Moran's henchmen. Soon, he'll be arrested, and his men with him. The problem, though, is…my late husband's family. I contacted them, but never received an answer.'

'I don't understand. Why are they a problem?'

'Three years ago, they paid Moran to kidnap Klara and kill me. There's no proof of that as long as Moran is at large. Moran has lost credibility with them and it seems they've turned away from him, but I need to be certain that he's not working for them anymore. And that they aren't employing some other killer to get what they want.'

'Do they know where you live?'

I shook my head. I hoped they didn't know, but I couldn't be sure.

Quinn's gaze grew unfocused. His brow fell into creases. 'Do you have a photograph of him?'

'I do.'

'I'll need a copy. If the detective you talked about loses him, or if you find out he's coming here, I'll show his face to…acquaintances. He won't set foot in Boston.'

I wasn't sure I was ready to trust him with my safety but nodded anyway.

Quinn folded his hands on his lap and changed the topic. 'A more detailed description of the dead man will be published in the papers tomorrow morning. I hope someone comes forward to identify him.'

Margery walked out onto the porch with a tray and set out a small dinner on the table. She retreated without a word. Did she taste the strange tension in the air?

'Why did you stay away for three months?' I asked abruptly.

The change of topic didn't seem to faze him. If anything, he had been waiting for the question.

'You put yourself at great risk to help me catch a murderer. You almost died, because I didn't trust your judgment. I'd treated you most foully. I was an ass, and yet you offered free treatment to Miss Hacker and her son, and to my daughter. You helped all of us and never asked for anything in return. I felt like I'd taken advantage of you, and thought it better to stay away for a while.'

'Interesting.'

'What?'

'I believed that you disappeared because it didn't matter to you. That you were used to people risking their lives for you, and you risking yours for them. You are a policeman after all. I believed that, perhaps, saving my life meant... nothing to you.'

His jaw worked as his eyes travelled from Líadáin's sleeping form up to my face. 'You made it clear that when the case was solved, you didn't want to see hide nor hair of me. It was a reasonable request at the time.'

We fell silent. The food was untouched. Líadáin's eyes flitted back and forth beneath her lids.

'You are wrong,' he said hoarsely. 'It matters to me.'

'elephone! Telephooooone! Te-le-pho-hone!'

'Yes, I hear it loud and clear!' Zachary shouted over Klara's screeching and the ringing of the dreadful thing. Merely an hour had passed since the telephone company had installed it, and already I wanted to rip the damned contraption off the wall.

'You have reached the Arlington Mansion. How may I help you?' Zach's nasal interpretation of a butler's voice and his pinky poking the air made me snort.

Boxing his shoulder, I snatched the receiver from him. 'Dr Elizabeth Arlington here.'

'Is this the home of Dr Arlington?' a woman hollered in my ear.

'Yes! This *is* Dr Elizabeth Arlington,' I shouted back. There was a lot of crackling and hissing. 'Who is there?'

'Inspector McCurley from the Boston Police Department wishes to speak to you. I will connect you now.'

More crackling and hissing. My eardrum was beginning to hurt.

'Elizabeth?'

'Yes! Quinn, is that you? You sound like you're drowning.'

'What did you say?'

'You sound like… Never mind.' My throat was raw from all the shouting. I hated telephoning. 'What did you want to tell me?'

'We have an identification. Could you come by my office at four in the afternoon?'

'I have a patient at three. Is four-thirty or five all right?'

'Yes! I'll see you then.' With a loud *crack*, Quinn was gone. I stared at the earpiece and shook my head.

HATTIE WAS a good friend and one of the few patients I had kept seeing regularly after I'd closed my practice. She was nine months pregnant with twins and spent most of her days lying on her side and complaining about the size of her stomach, her engorged breasts, and the many stretch marks that had begun appearing eight weeks earlier. Every time I examined her and listened to her laboured breathing, I was glad I had only one child.

'I wish I could go to the beach,' she grunted. 'This heat is killing me. But I'm sure people would think I was a stranded whale, and try to roll me back in.'

I laughed. My hands skimmed over her swollen abdomen, brushing baby bottoms, feet, and elbows. And there, a head. There was no space left for the two to bounce about. And so they kicked harder in protest.

Hattie stifled a burp. 'Excuse me. God, this heartburn. Why the deuce did Robert put *two* in my belly? Men are greedy creatures.'

'He put millions of sperm cells into your womb. You supplied two eggs. Or one, if they are identical twins.' I tickled her belly button.

'Gah! Your medical talk is disgusting, Liz!' She slapped my hand away. 'That gherkin joke you told us at Warren's bachelor ball *still* makes me shudder when I think of it. See!' She pointed at her stomach where gooseflesh rippled her skin.

'Well, it was pretty close to reality—'

'Let's change the subject. Will you come to our next meeting? The Freaks will come here, obviously. I can't roll all the way to Warren's. Do you even know where he lives now? Never mind. You won't visit him anyway.'

I cocked my head, wondering how much Warren had told his sister about his interest in me. But Hattie being Hattie, I didn't have long to wait for that piece of information.

'He's still…enamoured of you.' She rolled her eyes to the ceiling. 'God knows why.'

'Excuse me?'

Her gaze shifted back to me. 'He fancies sweet women, not…wild ones. I mean, look at you.' She waved a hand up and down my frame. 'Do you *ever* wear a skirt these days? And your hair, for Christ's sake! You gave me a shock when you walked in.'

'You don't like it?' I smirked and plucked at short curls that didn't even cover my ears.

Hattie opened her mouth and shut it. Opened it again. Clicked it shut. And huffed. 'One day you'll be arrested for pretending to be a man.'

'I'm not pretending to be a man!' Luckily, those days were over. 'And there's no law prohibiting the wearing of trousers, nor is it forbidden to cut my hair short. Several of my colleagues dress similarly. And don't forget the thousands of Boston women who wear knickerbockers for bicycling.'

She shook her head. 'Well, whatever you do, just don't break my brother's heart.'

'Hm.'

'Don't you *hm* me, Elizabeth Arlington!' Her index finger hovered close to my nose. 'Yes, he told me you aren't awfully interested in returning his feelings, but do me the favour and try not to be the bull in a china shop.'

My father had called me *an elephant in the china store*. On several occasions. 'I'm just being honest with Warren.'

She grunted again and rubbed her belly. 'Can I put my clothes back on?'

'Yes. We're done.' I helped her sit up, and laced the maternity corset loosely on her sides.

'Would you like to stay for tea?' she asked.

'I can't. I'm meeting Inspector McCurley.'

'Warren told me you're investigating a crime.'

'Hm-hmm.'

She squinted at me. 'Now I am worried.'

I waved her away, but she snatched my wrist. 'Liz, the last time you chased a killer you almost got yourself killed. I hope you aren't trying to catch one now. You aren't, are you?'

I cleared my throat. 'We're trying to identify a man.'

'Is he insane? Mute?'

'Dead.'

'You are joking, right? No, of course you aren't.' Hattie rubbed her brow and took a deep breath. 'I was so worried when I saw what Uriel's brother-in-law did to you. I didn't understand why you put yourself in such danger. And I still don't understand it. And now you...you're doing it again? You are a *mother*, Liz! Don't you even think of Klara?'

Her hands fisted in her lap, her fingers trembling. Softly, I put my hand over hers. 'Hattie, what I'm telling you now can't leave this room.'

She produced a small hiccup. I knew she'd tell Warren and perhaps Uriel. But that was all right with me, as long as she didn't spread it all over Boston's high society.

'I've been investigating crimes for years,' I said.

'What?'

'I never precisely set out to do detective work. It was more like I...stumbled into it.'

'*Stumbled* into it?'

'Yes. But that's not important. What I meant to tell you is that you don't need to worry, because I know what I'm doing.'

'You are a woman,' Hattie hissed. 'A mother. You have responsibilities.'

'Yes. That I do. And that's why I'm keeping my daughter safe. Do you think that nothing bad ever happens to the well-behaved women and girls?'

'Well, surely they—'

'Ugh, stop it, Hattie! Or else I'll have to conclude that you believe all murder victims somehow have it coming.'

'I think you should get married.'

Appalled, I threw up my hands. 'I have an appointment. Call me if you feel your pains coming.'

'I'm sorry, Liz. I shouldn't have said that. No one has the right to pressure you into marrying when you are still mourning your late husband. I'm just pointing out that three years is a long time.'

I shut my eyes and counted to three. I wasn't mourning my late husband. I was glad to be rid of him.

I put a smile on my face, told Hattie not to worry herself, and left.

I GREETED the constable at the front desk with a nod, and climbed the stairs to Quinn's office. I found him standing in the corridor, talking with another policeman.

'Go on in, I'll be there in a minute,' he said, motioning toward his office door.

I entered and walked up to the window to open it.

'This heat isn't natural,' Quinn said, as he rushed in and slammed the door shut. He yanked off his hat and wiped his brow on his shirt sleeve. Something dark shone through the white fabric.

'Is that a tattoo on your arm?'

Irritated, he scanned his sleeve. 'Is there a hole there I'm not seeing?'

'No. I thought I saw a black pattern through the fabric on your upper arm when you wiped your brow. But I can't see it now.'

He took his jacket off the peg by the door, and shrugged it on.

I gave him a puzzled look. He must be sweltering.

'If anyone here saw that, there'd be a lot of questions,' he explained without looking at me.

'Does it have to do with your past as a pit fighter?'

He cleared his throat, nodding once.

'The police catalogues tattoos of...infamous individuals. Would yours be familiar to them?'

His gaze flattened.

I thought back to what my friend, Uriel, had told me when I first met Quinn. He'd warned me that Quinn couldn't be trusted. The press called him *The Pit Bull*. Who had come up with that name?

'May I ask what it depicts? Your tattoo?'

'A serpent. It's how I strike.'

Ah, Quinn must have fed a fake *nome de guerre* to the newspapermen. A distraction. I wondered about his past and if his real name was still muttered in the fighting pits. Heat rose to my face as I tried to picture a snake curling up his chest. 'You are hiding in plain sight,' I said, leant back and grasped the windowsill, realising with surprise, 'It doesn't bother you anymore. I'm standing at the window and you're not... I'm sorry. I shouldn't have said that.'

What was wrong with my mouth today?

With a sigh, he pulled his revolver from his holster and placed it on the desk. 'It's taken me long enough to realise that very few people feel the urge to jump out of a window when they come by one.'

He pinched the bridge of his nose, and sat on the corner of his desk. 'I just had an interesting conversation with Sergeant Davies, and hope you can provide some insights.' He thrust his chin toward the corridor. 'Davies is the man I was talking to in the hallway. He reported that two new soup kitchens opened in Wards Six and Seven about a month ago, right among the most destitute and crowded blocks. Prices are *half* what the other soup kitchens charge. And they offer pasteurised milk in clean bottles to mothers who can't feed their babies. *Free* of charge. Do you happen to know anything about that?'

I cleared my throat. 'Why do you ask?'

He raked his fingers through his hair. Sweaty tufts stood up at the back of his neck. 'It's highly suspicious. That business can't be legitimate. They have to make a profit with *something*. Sergeant Davies and Detective Parks have searched the basements of both houses but found nothing. No fighting pit, no gambling or opium den. Apparently, an Englishman who lives in London is renting the premises. And a man named Smith is the steward, but he communicates with the landlord only by letter. Would you mind asking your patients if they've heard anything next time you visit the Wards?'

I pushed my hands into my trouser pockets. 'There's nothing illicit about those two soup kitchens.'

'Huh.' A sharp glance, and then he picked up a pencil and began worrying it with a clasp knife. Narrow shavings tumbled to the floor. 'You know something, but you don't want to tell me.'

I shrugged a shoulder.

'The Boston Police Department opened an investigation. They'll raid those kitchens whenever they raid the rum cellars and saloons in the neighbourhood.' He placed the sharp pencil on the desk and picked up another one. 'That's three, four times a week.'

'They won't find anything.'

'Are you involved?'

I lifted an eyebrow.

His knuckles whitened. The pencil crackled under the pressure of the blade. Abruptly, he sat up straight. 'The handwriting of the steward seemed familiar. I just couldn't put my finger on it until now. Why would *you* be posing as the steward?'

'I will tell you if you promise this won't leave your office.'

Grunting, he blew pencil shrapnel from his trousers, and leant back. 'If there's anything illegal about that business, I can't keep it to myself. I'm a policeman.'

'And if the soup kitchens are wholly legitimate?'

'In that case, I...will keep my mouth shut.'

I ran a finger along the windowsill, picked up a dead fly and threw it out. 'They are mine.'

He spluttered. 'You *own* the soup kitchens?'

I nodded.

'That must cost you...what? Fifty dollars per month?'

'Fifty gallons of milk, plus vegetables and meat for approximately three hundred fifty to four hundred meals per day, plus the costs for crockery and glass bottles, wood, coal, wages, and the like all amount to roughly two-hundred fifty dollars per month for both kitchens.'

He blinked. If he hadn't already been sitting, I was sure his knees would have gone soft. 'How can you possibly...

Why would you… And in the Black Sea district of all places! You will go bankrupt if you keep this up.'

I shook my head. 'My husband left me some money.'

He narrowed his eyes. 'And you don't want to invest it?'

'Isn't that what I'm doing? I'm putting it to good use. It feeds people and keeps babies alive.'

Quinn's expression fell. 'And we are raiding your soup kitchens.'

I waved a dismissive hand. 'I can't go policing them myself, and I'm sure they'd morph into opium dens at some point without occasional police intervention.'

I turned away to gaze out the window and into Pemberton Square. A cabbie was softly muttering to his horse as he brushed it down and watered it.

'About your inheritance…' He paused, searching for words.

My heart sank. 'You want to know how much it is.'

'No. I just…don't want others to take advantage of your kindness. Will you let me know if your money runs out? Will you promise to ask for help?'

My heart beat like a cricket. A smile warmed my face. Strange, it was always those who had to make do with very little who offered help. They knew what it meant to have nothing. Quinn was struggling to make ends meet, yet he was offering financial aid. 'I promise I will if you will promise me the same. To ask me for help.'

He inclined his head.

In a whisper, I added, 'And I thank you for your kind offer. But it won't be necessary. I could run ten of those kitchens for the rest of my life.'

He opened his mouth, then shut it and turned his gaze away.

'What?'

'How did your husband die?' The question was fired like a bullet from his mouth.

Ah. I knew I shouldn't have hinted at the sheer size of my inheritance. 'Is that the inspector asking?'

Upon my incredulous stare, he lifted his hands. 'No. It's a friend asking. I'm not insinuating… I just… I want to know what you've gone through. But I realise now that I have no right to ask. Please accept my apologies.'

I scanned his face. The prominent scar running from cheek to throat. The thunderstorm blue eyes. He turned his face away just a fraction, showing the unmarred side. Had he been doing that for a while now?

'I killed him.'

He reared back. 'W…what? Why?'

'He was a murderer.'

His jaw was working, but he made an effort to keep his expression undemanding, trying not to pressure me into giving him information I didn't wish to give freely. But his resolve broke. 'You could not go to the police?'

'No, I could not.' I took a step closer to him, lifted my right hand — the one with the missing index finger — and touched my knuckles to the jagged scar that must have nearly cost Quinn's life. 'Who gave you this?'

His eyes flared.

I dropped my hand.

He bent forward, and said softly, 'There will be no information trade. We left that behind us. If you want to know about that injury, I will tell you how it happened, whether or not you tell me about your husband.'

I gave him a small nod.

'This…' he motioned at the scar, '…happened during a pit fight. Right after, actually. My opponent lay in the sand. I believed him unconscious. He wasn't. He snatched a bottle from a man in the crowd, broke off the bottom, and slashed me. He couldn't accept defeat. He'd been bested by a boy half his size.'

I had no words.

'I was lucky. The wound was deep, laying free the artery, but not nicking it. When I put my hand there, it felt like a wet, pounding snake.'

I sucked in a hiss. 'The wound wasn't stitched up by a physician, was it?'

He shook his head. 'No. The man who owned me did it.'

'What? You were—'

'Property. Yes. But that's a long story. I'll tell you another time if you want to know.'

'I...do.'

His gaze dropped to my lips, and lingered there, igniting a fire in my belly.

A knock sounded. We drew back from one another.

Quinn called, 'Come in.'

Boyle stuck his head around the door frame. 'I just got word that your court appointment is scheduled for nine o'clock tomorrow morning. The Millers case.'

'Thank you, Sergeant.' With a nod, Quinn dismissed him, and clapped a hand to his knee. 'Late this morning, a woman came in and identified the Mystic River man. We showed her photographs of the corpse and drawings of old injuries to his skin and bones. Based on the shape of the man's ears, an old fracture to his shin, a scar on his forearm, the colour of his hair, his height, and his teeth she recognised the body as that of her husband, Charles Hartwell.'

'Was he in your files as a missing person?'

'No. He was never reported missing. He lived apart from his wife and three children whenever he went on a "chase," as Mrs Hartwell called it. He was an investigative journalist. Interestingly, he knew sign language. His brother was deaf.'

'Was?'

'He died of pneumonia as a boy. Mrs Hartwell told us that her husband occasionally worked for the *Boston Post*, so I caught the editor during his lunch break and asked a few questions. He stated that Mr Hartwell's "style" wasn't appreciated by his colleagues, but as long as the man delivered stories that sold, he'd been kept on payroll.'

'Why did no one miss him?'

'Charles Hartwell was known to go undercover. He would disappear for weeks on end to investigate a story. This time, he was gone for more than six weeks. The editor confessed that it was a bit long, even for Hartwell. If he hadn't returned or sent a note in the next few days, the editor would have contacted Hartwell's wife.'

'What was he working on?' I asked.

'No one seems to know.'

'Strange. Do you believe that?'

'Of course not.'

'So Hartwell worked on a story for a month, at some point he met Arthur, and someone caught wind of whatever he was investigating and killed him?'

Quinn scratched his scar absentmindedly, and again turned the marred side of his face away from me. 'Seems probable. The medical examiners found small metal shavings in Arthur's clothes. I'm beginning to think that our theory of illegal child labour has merit.'

'Margery said something the other day,' I threw in. 'She told me that she's making an effort to send Arthur out to play and read with Klara. He's terrified of not working fast enough, and even more terrified when he makes a mistake.'

'Have you found scarring that would indicate—'

'That he'd been whipped? No. But taking a switch to palms of his hands or soles of his feet wouldn't leave marks as long the skin isn't broken. Margery said he was hiding his hands when he dropped a jar. The whole boy was trembling when it shattered.'

Quinn rubbed his stubbly jaw. 'All right. I'll have Boyle dig through reports from The Bureau of Statistics of Labor and the Board of Health. Anything that points to factories being fined for employing underage children. Were you able to get any more information from the boy?'

I sagged against the window sash. 'We can't expect him to communicate fluently any time soon. Miss Lowell spent three hours with the children today. She says that Arthur knows only a handful of signs. He's a sharp one, but it's still a completely new language he's learning, and that will take time. So I asked him to draw me his home and his family. He didn't know what I was talking about. He did, however, make a drawing of the man, Charles Hartwell, and the place they went to skip stones. A river. He nodded when I asked him if it was Mystic River. But I'm not sure if he just wanted to please me with that answer. I'll ask him after dinner tonight to draw some more. And we'll go skipping stones. Do you want to come?'

My heart dropped as his expression darkened.

Hastily, I added, 'I understand, of course, if you'd rather not. You know now what I...did.'

'I want to come,' he said, his voice somber. 'But there's something I don't understand. You tried very hard not to tell me that you feed the destitute, but you seemed to have no reservations telling me that you...killed your husband.'

'Because I can be connected with one, but not the other.'

'But you admitted to a killing. I'm a policeman. Why would you trust me with that?'

I coughed to get rid of the lump in my throat. 'Because you have begun to look at me differently. You've started hiding the scarred side of your face. You didn't like seeing Warren Amaury in my sitting room. You believe I'm...too good in some way because I treat the poor and feed them and don't ask for payment. I treated your daughter and didn't ask for payment. You were *bound* to get a wrong impression of me.'

'You just lied about your husband, told me you killed him so that I stop looking at you differently?'

'No, I…like the way you look at me.' I was surprised by my own admission. 'And I didn't lie about my husband. I hate that you think you need to hide your scar from me. But you are running blindly into…this. And I can't have that. You need to know that I plotted a murder. Meticulously. And I executed it.' My voice was a mere whisper. No one would be able to overhear us through the flimsy door.

His Adam's apple bobbed. 'That doesn't explain why you trust me with this. It could cost you your life.'

'No, it won't. It can't. There is no evidence, not even a grave. Mr Arlington never existed.'

10

I have to show you something,' Zach said when I returned home. He was blocking the hallway, his face a strained mask.

'What's wrong? Did Arthur run away again?'

'Not...yet.' He stepped aside to clear the view of the telephone on the wall.

'Oh...my...' I clapped a hand to my mouth.

The rim of the black, funnel-shaped mouthpiece was painted red. Each of the two circular brass bells above the mouthpiece sported a fat, black spot in the centre. And atop the telephone box itself lay a shoe-brush, its brown bristles poking up in the air, two pink ribbons attached and trailing down on either side.

'Well, that's...' I picked at the receiver that was hanging from its cord and decorated with a glove. 'She has only one hand. But that shouldn't impede her chances for a good marriage, what with those pretty lips and large, expressive eyes.'

Zach was wheezing with laughter.

'Does she have a name?'

'I have no idea. But Margery threatened to confiscate all of Klara's wax crayons for the next decade.' He wiped his eyes and gulped a deep breath.

'We should baptise her after dinner. But first, we should try and save the kids before they get drawn and quartered.'

'I heard that!' came from the kitchen.

∿

AFTER CEREMONIOUSLY NAMING OUR TELEPHONE "ROSIE," I took Klara and Arthur down to the cove. We raced each other barefoot through greyish white sand and kicked small rocks into the water. It didn't take long for the children to look like swamp monsters. Arthur kept his distance from the other people there, watching them all with sharp eyes. The boy was constantly placing himself between Klara and strangers, angling his body so that he could push the smaller girl out of the way from whatever threat might come from a grown-up. I yearned to take this weight off him. Yearned to know what had made him so protective.

I spotted Quinn sitting on a patch of grass, slipping off his shoes and socks, and rolling up his trousers.

'Sorry, am I late?' he said as he walked up to us.

I smiled. 'No. Skipping stones isn't precisely a time-sensitive activity.'

'The metal shavings we found on Arthur's clothes are copper with a small percentage of brass and iron. No furnace slag was found on them. What do you make of that?'

'Hum. He might have worked at a copper mine, far away from the furnaces? Or he was kept in a metal workshop.' I stopped myself. 'Did they say anything about the quality of the metals?'

A corner of his mouth curled. 'The iron shavings were

oxidised, but that's normal. The copper was high quality. Ninety-nine per cent pure.'

'Not ore, then.' I cocked my head. 'What game are you playing, Inspector McCurley?'

'I just wanted to know if you and I would arrive at the same conclusion.'

I snorted. 'I'm a physician, not a detective. But it's obvious now the boy didn't work at a mine. Are you looking for a place that cuts or drills into copper? That makes small parts, like…um, wires?'

He bobbed his head. 'High-quality copper is found in electronic appliances, lower quality in cook- and tableware. Boyle's made a list of workshops and factories we need to consider. It's a long list, but Haggots and Sons are of particular interest.'

He curled his toes into the sand. A faint scar on the side of his foot reminded me of the night he'd chased a convicted murderer, injured his foot, and missed a bullet by a mere inch. 'Sounds like you and Sergeant Boyle will be busy.'

'Why does that make you smile?' he asked softly.

I nodded at his bare feet. 'I just thought of the night you nearly ran me over, wearing only your nightshirt. Your toe has healed well.'

'That night is hard to forget.' He brushed the back of my hand with his. 'I never thanked you.'

That night, I'd probably saved his life. 'When I saw that man grab his revolver, my mind…switched off. Next thing I knew I was holding a smoking gun in my hand. I didn't even hear the report until after all was over. It wasn't a conscious decision to kill him.'

'Good reflexes are the result of excellent training.'

I shook my head. 'I'd rather not have the need for that.'

'No one wants to kill. But sometimes it's necessary to save a life.'

I lifted my eyes. His gaze held mine, rested in mine.

'Why Haggots and Sons?' I whispered.

He didn't move a muscle. 'Because they engrave printing plates in West Medford. Near the Mystic Lakes. The material and the location fit.'

'Isn't that outside your jurisdiction?'

He shook his head no. A deep frown carved his brow. His gaze lingered on my mouth.

'Are you mourning your wife?'

He took half a step back, pulling in a stuttering breath. 'You won't like to hear this.'

'Try me.'

'I don't think I ever grieved Ailis' death. At least that's how it feels. There was fury about what she'd done. *Endless* fury. And regret that I wasn't a better husband. I kept wondering what I'd done that broke her. Or was it just…our life that drove her over the edge? The fact that we were both lonely together?'

He washed a hand over his face and spoke to the dying sunset, the bruised sky. Not to me. 'I will never forgive her. She abandoned her child and her husband. Her family. Without a thought. She wanted to kill Líadáin. An innocent, defenceless newborn. She very nearly succeeded.'

A knife drawn from its sheath — that's how his voice sounded. In that moment, he seemed to turn away from the world, and into his private, walled-in space. A space I happened to be standing next to, listening to words he hadn't meant anyone to hear. Or didn't care whether anyone heard them.

And then he said, 'I stopped asking myself why.'

'She was…ill.' Damn, why was my voice failing now? 'It was not her fault. Nor was it yours.'

A stiffening of his shoulders.

I wanted to reach out and place a comforting hand on his

back. But I didn't. This wasn't the time. 'Illness of the mind is as serious and debilitating as illness of the body. But it is so much harder to understand, to see, and to cure. A broken leg can be mended. But a broken mind? Perhaps in a hundred years. Perhaps sooner. But until then, all we can do is listen and try our best.'

He said nothing, but he didn't move away either.

'What I mean to say is… She wasn't herself when she did it.'

His face was bare of all expression. I'd never seen such a void in a man.

I cleared the lump from my throat, and continued, 'The process of birth is…dramatic. The fear of dying is real. The body goes through drastic changes in a very short time. Most women deal with it just fine. But some fall ill, physically or… mentally. It's rare, but it happens. It's likely that your wife suffered from this illness, that her madness was brought on by the birth and death of your first child. And she never really recovered from it. And when her second child was born, it got worse.'

His nostrils flared. 'And you? Do you grieve?'

The question stunned me. 'How can you think I grieve that man? He abducted me and murdered my father.'

His jaw ticked. 'So why would you think I'd grieve the woman who wanted my daughter dead?' Then his gaze softened. 'But you grieve the person you were before you were forced to choose. Before you realised there was no right way, and all you can do is look back, and wonder *what if.*'

I wasn't sure whether he was referring to himself or me. Both, perhaps. I gave him a nod. 'Sometimes I wonder… about my coldness. What I'm capable of, if pushed, and… Where is Klara?' Alarmed that I had lost sight of her and couldn't hear her voice, I scanned the beach.

Quinn touched my shoulder and pointed to my left. 'She's right there with Arthur.'

I huffed with relief. 'You didn't bring Líadáin.'

'I came directly from Headquarters. And I have to leave now. I just…wanted to let you know about the copper.'

Silently, we walked to the patch of grass where he'd left his shoes and socks. As he pulled them on, I asked, 'What was the real reason you stayed away for three months?'

He stood and looked me square in the eye. 'The same as yours. I wasn't brave enough.'

11

I still felt the soft sand between my toes, when the children and I brushed off our shoes on the doormat, and entered the house. Margery sat at the kitchen table mending a shirt, and Zachary was bent over our financial records.

He lifted his gaze and waved a pencil at me. 'Here's what we spent last month. It's more than May and June together. It's making me nervous.'

'Don't be. We're good.'

'You didn't even look at the numbers,' he grumbled.

'As long as you don't buy a house behind my back, we're fine.'

Margery placed her sewing flat on the table. 'Why do you ask him to do the bookkeeping if you don't care how much we spend?'

'I didn't ask him. He said he wanted to do it, and I told him it's not absolutely necessary. He does it anyway.' I shrugged.

Margery squeezed her eyes shut, struggling for patience.

A small elbow bumped my side. Arthur beamed up at me,

then pointed to the accounts book. I looked at Zach. 'May he take a look?'

Zachary pushed the volume across the table. Arthur indicated the pencil. Zach handed it to him. Reverently, the boy grasped both items, then knelt on the floor in a patch of electric light. With a flourish, he drew a squiggle smack in the middle of a page, hopped to his feet and excitedly pointed at it.

I frowned at him. He was grinning from ear to ear, utterly proud of himself.

I tried a smile. 'What is it?'

He picked up the book, placed it back on the table, and tapped his finger to the squiggle. I still didn't know what it was. It looked just like a signature, but that couldn't be. A six-year-old wouldn't write his family name with such flourish. Besides, Arthur could neither read nor write. But perhaps…

'You wrote someone's name?'

Blinking, he poked out his lower lip and looked for Klara.

'Want to read about King Arthur?' she asked. A grin and a nod, and off they went.

Zach snatched his book and went back to bookkeeping.

'Do you know what he wanted to tell us?' I asked him.

'No idea.'

'Hum.' Puzzled, I followed the children, and found them sitting on my bed, bent over a tome. 'Oh no you don't! Wash before you hop on my bed, you swamp monsters.'

'One more!'

One more chapter. It was always one more chapter. I couldn't be mad at her for that. But I tried to plaster a stern look on my face anyway. 'No discussions, young lady. And you, too, young man. Go, wash. I'll… Damn.' As they scooted off my bed, I found several handfuls of sand and muck on my blanket. But Klara and Arthur cleared the room before I could say a peep. Next thing I heard was a screech from the bathroom. 'Mamaaaaa! Arthur has a noodle!'

I stuffed a pillow in my face and laughed.

∼

THREE DAYS LATER, Quinn showed up on my doorstep. He ripped off his hat. 'A thunderstorm is brewing. It's about time we had some rain.'

I looked over his shoulder at the black wall approaching from the sea. 'Come in.'

'Thank you, but a police carriage is waiting. I just wanted to let you know that we found Arthur's orphanage. It *seems* we did, I should say. A deaf boy of about Arthur's age, with the same colour hair and eyes, was adopted four months ago by a Mr and Mrs Tillmann of 21 Bennington Street, East Boston. The problem is that no one at 21 Bennington Street has ever heard of the Tillmanns.'

'The name sounds German.'

'They didn't have an accent according to the headmaster of the orphanage. It was the only thing he remembered about them.'

'Do you want me to ask around? Ward One isn't my usual beat. People probably won't talk to me.'

He shook his head. 'Not necessary. I have two officers on the case. But I need to take the boy to the orphanage and to Bennington Street. See if he recognises someone.'

'You want to take him right away?'

'In two days. I'd appreciate if I could borrow his drawings until then. Anything that might depict his home or the place where he was working.'

'I've got a whole stack in my office, but I'm not sure how helpful they'll be. Wait a moment.'

As I returned with a dozen drawings rolled up and tied

with a string, the first heavy drops of rain splattered onto the dusty doormat. Quinn put his hat back on and hunched his shoulders.

'Would you like an umbrella?'

'No, thank you. There's one in the carriage. I'll be around tomorrow, but I'll be staying out of sight, see if anyone is loitering in the area.' He stuffed the drawings into his jacket, tapped a finger to the rim of his hat, and left.

'Thank you,' I muttered.

Tomorrow, Klara would turn three.

My insides churned.

~

THE HEAVY RAIN continued into the next day. Klara didn't mind. In fact, she and Arthur were happy about every deep puddle on the premises. They even pretended fishing in the biggest one.

I didn't mind the weather, either. The conditions for a sharpshooter were less favourable with the visibility so low. He'd have to get closer to us, and that meant Quinn, Zach, and I would have a better chance to spot him. I knew Moran was in Europe. Still, my nerves were pulled taut, and my senses stretched far. I wish I knew where Quinn was. If he was really keeping an eye on Klara, as he'd promised.

Of course he would be close by. He wasn't one to back out of promises.

It felt strange to have to trust him with this. Like jumping from a low bridge, and not quite knowing if the water below was deep enough for the dive.

I stood at the bay window, gazing into the downpour. The two children were dark outlines, flitting to and fro in the rain. There was no real need for me to keep an eye on them because Zach was standing watch on the porch, his revolver in his pocket. I'd relieve him after lunch.

I laughed when Klara "fell" into a particularly large puddle for the umpteenth time, and Arthur offered his hand to help her up, just to "stumble" into the muck right next to her. They'd been playing that game for more than two hours. I wasn't worried about them catching a cold. The rain and the ground were warm enough.

Margery signalled her disapproval by huffing every time she walked past a window and caught sight of the children. But she held her tongue. Children need to play and get dirty, to climb and fall and hurt themselves. I couldn't imagine locking them in the house, forcing them to sit still and look neat all day long.

Klara ran up to the window and pressed her nose to it, grinning up at me. Arthur followed in her wake. She lifted her hands and signed, 'H-A-L-L-O.' Her short fingers slowly forming each letter. They'd been practising every day. Miss Lowell had given them colourful sheets with sign alphabet and a few dozen words in sign language. Depending on their mood, the children pretended it was a secret language that no one but the two of them understood, or one that only our family understood.

Did Arthur think of us as his family? No, certainly not. There was too much mistrust in the boy. Except... Except for Klara. He trusted her completely. He was her shadow. There was never a flinch or a flattening of his gaze when she yelled her usual "BUT I WANT TO!" at him.

Klara began to sign again, but got confused and argued with Arthur about which sign was the correct one. Then they simply waved at me to come join them. Two sets of eyes followed my fingers as I signed, 'Y-E-S.'

We had Klara's favourite food for lunch — Tyrolean dumplings, modified by Margery to fit a bit more fried ham and garlic into the delectable packages. I still felt stuffed from the strawberry cream cake we'd had for breakfast. Arthur hadn't been able to contain himself at the sight of it. Worried someone would take it from him, he'd shoved a monstrous piece into his mouth, smearing cream from the tip of his chin to the base of his nose. His eyes had bulged when Margery dumped a second piece onto his plate.

He was trying to push an entire dumpling past his teeth when Rosie rang.

'Yes?' Margery barked into the mouthpiece. 'One moment, please.' She gave me the receiver and I was connected to…

'This is Angie, Mrs Heathcote's personal maid. Dr Arlington, you must come quickly, my mistress' water broke! Mr Heathcote just sent a carriage.' The connection broke with a loud *crack*.

'Margery, fetch my bag. It's packed and ready on my desk. Zach, find the inspector and bring him here.' I rushed to the bathroom to rub the rain from my hair.

Earlier, Zachary had found Quinn down by the boathouses, and tried to convince him to take lunch with us. But without success. Now that I had to leave to attend to Hattie, I hoped he wouldn't refuse to come in out of the rain and eat a bite.

A few moments later, Hattie's carriage arrived with clattering wheels. I waited until a drenched Quinn entered through the backdoor along with Zach. He saw the tension in my shoulders and gave me a reassuring nod.

And then I was gone.

Robert Heathcote, Hattie's husband, stood guard in front

of her private rooms. I'd rarely seen him. He was usually away on business trips or attending social events.

His eyes touched upon my short hair and narrowed. As if my haircut had any bearing on my skills as a physician. I said hello, stepped around him into the room, and snapped the door shut behind me. Hattie lay on her side, a gaggle of maids surrounding her. Everyone was wringing their hands. This looked more like an overcrowded chicken coop than a birthing chamber.

'Thank God you're here,' Hattie groaned.

I touched her clammy forehead, leant in and whispered, 'What are all these people doing here?'

She snorted. 'Attending to me, of course.'

'Your water broke?'

She nodded and curled into an oncoming contraction. I watched her, gauging the intensity of her labour. She seemed all right. A bit pale, perhaps. And very tense.

'Leave us,' I told the servants. Their eyes flicked to Hattie, who flapped her hands at them, waving them off.

'When was the last time you ate and drank?' I asked.

'Mothers in labour aren't supposed to. Shouldn't *you* of all people know that?'

I checked my watch as I placed my bag on the nightstand. 'That's nonsense, you know. The no-food policy. Any explosive bowel movements yet? Have you been sick?'

She touched her brow. 'How could I...did I forget that? Is something wrong with my mind, Liz? I've given birth twice and didn't remember the... Well, you know the... Until just now.'

'Vomiting and diarrhoea.'

'Yes, that. I probably called for you too early, too, didn't I?'

I patted her hip. 'No, you didn't. Your water broke. Let me see how far along you are.'

'I don't think a head is sticking out already. I'd feel that.'

I grinned. 'I'm going to check your cervix. The closer to birth you are, the more dilated it is.' I stood to wash my hands and roll up my sleeves.

'My what?' That was when the next contraction came on. Six minutes from the previous one. Both seemed to pain her greatly. With disdain, I thought of her old physician, the one who had *attended* Hattie's previous births from the other side of the bedroom door, while a midwife had hollered at Hattie to pull herself together.

I waited for the contraction to subside, then placed my warm hands on Hattie's abdomen. 'Let's get this corset off. And the skirts.'

The maternity corset was soft and comfortable, but she needed unrestricted mobility for what was to come. I got her into a nightgown and robe, then helped her move onto her side. I angled up her thigh and probed with two fingers. Her cervix to be half-dilated. She still had a few hours, it seemed.

'Are you hungry?' I asked.

'I could eat a cow. And I'm parched.'

'Let's go to the kitchens, then.'

'You're joking!'

'No, I'm not. You need sustenance, and you need to move your hips. Help the babies along. Now, up with you, Mrs Heathcote.' I pulled on her arm and helped her sit up.

'What if the pain comes?' There was naked fear in her voice. She was used to lying prone for hours in giving birth, to letting it happen to her, not taking an active part in the process.

'Then you lean on me. Come on. Stand up.'

WE MADE it down to the kitchens with two contractions and a lot of huffing and grunting. The kitchen staff exploded into activity when we entered. I sent all but one of the cooks away.

'Chicken coop,' I muttered, which tickled a laugh from Hattie.

'It's getting worse,' she groaned, as she leant against a chopping block. 'Oh gods, it's getting worse.'

'Good. That means I get back home in time for supper.'

As soon as she had recovered from the contraction, she boxed my arm. 'Elizabeth Arlington, you are a brute! But I love you anyway.'

'May I remind you that *you* were the one harping that you couldn't wait to pop them out?'

'God, my back is killing me.' She shuffled over to a chair and sank down. Cook put a cup of tea and a plate of cold beef slices in front of her. Hattie gulped down the tea, looked at the food, and mumbled, 'I'm going to be sick.'

'Let's find a bathroom for you.' The trip down the stairs had sped up her labour nicely. We reached the bathroom and I held her as she emptied her stomach and bowels. I didn't need to check her cervix to know she must be almost fully dilated.

'While I get you cleaned up, you can decide where you want to give birth. It'll happen soon, and if you want to get back to your rooms, we have to leave now.'

She only nodded. Sweat was dripping from her temples.

I recruited two maids to get Hattie up the two flights of stairs and into bed, then sent them off immediately sent them with "tasks" — the usual water boiling and towel heating. It would keep them too busy to intrude on us. Birthing was best done in peace, and a gaggle of hand-wringers was the last thing one needed in *any* situation.

Hattie's contractions were coming quick and powerful now. She took each with clenched teeth and high-pitched shrieks.

'Hattie, do yourself a favour and rail at me, would you?'

'Wh...at?'

'Stop lying still. Stop being quiet. Stop holding everything in. You want it all to come out. You have two babies that want out.'

'What do you want me to do?'

'I want to hear the filthiest language you can think of.'

She burst out laughing. The laugh rolled into a contraction.

I grasped her hand. 'You are a brute, Elizabeth Arlington,' I prompted her.

'You are a brute, Elizabeth Arlington!' she cried half-heartedly.

'All right. Maybe I'm not the best target. It's my charms, I suppose. What about Robert? The *bastard* that put them in your belly.' I winked at her.

Her eyes flared. She curled her hands to fists. 'Robert... you INGRATE...I'll cut off your...BLOODY GODDAMN BALLS...AH! I'll smash them with a HAMMER! One! After! THE OTHER!'

'That was a good contraction! You can push with the next one if you want to.'

'I'm exhausted,' she mumbled and shut her eyes.

I let her rest for two minutes, but when the next contraction came, I said, 'Enough with being comfortable. You've got work to do. Your babies want to be born. Squat, Hattie.'

She *did* work then. And boy, did she rail at me, at her husband, at her painful back, at the rain hammering against the windows and the carpets looking so dull. At some point, I handed her a vase which she smashed against the wall. And with a mighty shout, the first of the twins slipped into my waiting palms.

*A*round nine o'clock in the evening, I unlocked the door to our house. Low voices came from the kitchen. I followed them and found Zachary and Quinn sitting at the table, a bottle of rum and a pot of what smelled like coffee between them. They looked up when I leant against the doorframe.

'I'll leave, then,' both said at the same time. There was an awkward moment of silence.

Zach gave me a smile and mumbled that he'd be off to bed to sleep off "all that rum."

Amused, I huffed. He rarely drank, and if he did, he couldn't stomach more than two shots. Quinn stood and picked up his hat from the backrest of a chair. The usually dark grey felt was black with rainwater.

'You don't drink,' I said, pointing at his coffee cup. It wasn't a question. He grew up in a slum among alcoholics. His father had killed his mother in a stupor. No doubt he hated what alcohol did to people.

'No, I don't.' He paused.

'I was just...' he said, just as I said, 'Thank you for...'

We blinked at one another.

'Let's sit for a moment?' I suggested.

He sat back down.

'Thank you for keeping my family safe.' I poured myself a sip of rum into Zach's empty coffee cup.

'How is Mrs Heathcote doing?'

'Hmm.' I rolled the drink around in my mouth, shut my eyes for a moment and leant back in my chair. 'She's doing well. She had two sons. Identical twins.' I smiled. Stupidly, most likely.

He cocked his head. 'You seem…different tonight.'

'Birth is…hard to put into words. If you let it, if you give a mother the freedom to do what her body commands, and lend her your strength, show her her own strength, she transforms into a lioness. To be a part of that is…powerful.'

Silence fell. All that was, was two people looking at one another. Seeing each other. Quinn opened his mouth to speak but shut it quickly. His eyes darted to the clock on the wall. 'I need to leave.'

'I know,' I whispered.

'I'd like you to come with us tomorrow.'

'Of course. I'm curious, too, and I won't send Arthur by himself. I'll take Klara, as well. He trusts her more than he trusts me. If he trusts me at all. What precisely have you planned? I can't agree to this if the child is put in danger.'

His expression darkened.

'I'm sorry. I didn't mean to make you think that…that I…' I groaned and rubbed my eyes. 'I'm sorry.'

'You look exhausted. You should go to bed.'

I pushed my rum aside.

His chair scraped across the floorboards as he stood. 'I'll pick you up at ten in the morning.'

Unspeaking, I accompanied him to the door, watched

him pick up his mackintosh and methodically fold it over his arm. Watched him search for words that didn't come.

In the doorway, he paused, his head lowered. 'I talked to a few acquaintances. People who owe me a favour. They'll keep their ears open for anyone asking for a British or German woman physician.'

'How much did you tell them?'

'Nothing. Only what I just said.' His voice sounded hollow. 'Good night, Elizabeth.'

∾

AT TEN O'CLOCK the next morning Quinn was back. Sergeant Boyle waited by the black police carriage. Another sergeant perched on the driver's seat, chewing on a cigarette.

'I'm sorry for...' Quinn and I blurted out simultaneously.

Klara bumped into my legs, and flitted outside, closely followed by Arthur. While she ran ahead to talk to Boyle, Arthur stopped halfway, undecided.

'Did you talk to the boy?' Quinn asked.

I nodded. I'd told Arthur earlier that the police needed him to look at houses and people from afar. I assured him he could stay in the carriage with Klara and me. He could help the police find the persons who killed his friend Charles Hartwell by simply pointing out of the carriage window whenever someone or something looked familiar.

'Three policemen? Isn't that a bit much?' I asked.

'If Arthur spots anything that's familiar to him, Boyle will knock on the roof. Sergeant Masters will take you and the children a safe distance away while Boyle and I investigate.' Quinn's gaze slid to where a holster lay hidden against my thigh. An appreciative nod, then he took a step back, approached Arthur and squatted down in front of him.

I grabbed my umbrella from the stand by the door, and

followed. My mouth was full of words, but there was no opportunity to utter them. Since we'd spoken the night before, I'd wanted to tell Quinn that I was sorry. I shouldn't have talked about birth the way I had, given his own terrible experience with it. What I'd described as beautiful, was deepest sadness and loss to him.

But what *he* might wish to apologise for, I had not the slightest clue.

'Are you ready to go?' he asked the boy.

Arthur nodded once, his chin trembling.

'Good,' Quinn said, briefly touched the boy's shoulder, and crossed our front yard to climb up on the driver's seat. I noticed the butt of a rifle peeking from under the seat. I knew that Quinn was carrying a revolver, so why the need for yet another weapon?

'You plan to go on a raid armed to the teeth with two small children tagging along? What the hell are you thinking?'

'Elizabeth, I promise you, it's safe. If it were necessary, I'd bring Líadáin. This—' he motioned at the carriage, '—is a sightseeing trip with well-armed guards. Neither the orphanage nor the Tillmanns are expecting us.' A little softer, he added, 'These people are not professional killers. They botched the murder of Hartwell. They won't be waiting for us with drawn guns. And even if Boyle and I need to open fire, you'll be far away. You and the children will just be driving past. None of you will be in any danger. I won't allow it.'

My jaw worked. The weight of my revolver against my leg felt reassuring. I gave Quinn a stiff nod, and climbed into the carriage where Arthur was watching Klara babble away cheerfully. Sergeant Boyle would nod at her, a smile curling his moustache.

I hoped I wouldn't regret this day.

We left Savin Hill and took Dorchester Avenue north to Ward Six. The East Boston's Ferry took us across the inlet. Grey clouds hung low, and light rain blanketed the water. The ferry rocked and rolled, and Klara giggled with joy. Gulls sat huddled on the railing, their calls sounding like complaints about the weather.

I pointed toward the wet basin at the Navy Yard. Arthur's gaze followed my finger to the schooner in the dock. His jaw unhinged as he produced a strange croaking noise of awe.

We lost sight of the large white sails as the ferry docked. Sergeant Masters clicked his tongue. Snorting, the two horses pulled us across the landing. The hollow clatter of wooden boards against the wheels of our carriage made the window pane jiggle in its frame. Arthur pressed a hand against it, and the other to the seat. He shut his eyes and tilted his head. I wondered if he would like to listen to music that way. Smack in the middle of an orchestra, with his fingers splayed on a drum skin.

As we turned into Bennington Street, I tapped his shoulder and pointed at the buildings. 'Have you been here before?'

Tension rolled through the boy at once. He gazed outside, blinked twice, his eyes large and full of trepidation. I waited for the moment of recognition, the abrupt lightening of expression, or the shutting down in shock and fear. None of that happened. We passed hawkers and secondhand clothes shops, a dustcart, and a group of playing children. All elicited interest from the boy, but little more.

The four-wheeler came to a halt at number twenty-one. 'Anything?' Quinn called down to us.

'No. Nothing yet,' Boyle replied.

'Onwards, then.'

The carriage lurched gently, and drove us through Ward One. Arthur looked out the window, with Klara pressed against his side, and nearly climbing onto his lap. She was pointing at people, shops, churches, and explaining with so many words what everything was. Or what she theorised they must be, because she'd never been there before. The sausage shop. The trousers shop. The hairbrush shop.

We took Meridian across Chelsea Creek, turned and crossed the water once more at Chelsea Bridge. Arthur's neck grew longer when we passed the Navy Yard from its opposite side. Klara pressed her button nose flat on the window.

All through Charlestown, the boy showed no sign of recognition.

A knock on the roof. 'Anyone hungry?' Quinn called down to us. 'The oysters at Waterman's Wharf are very good.'

Klara was always hungry these days, and whatever one offered to Arthur was devoured in a heartbeat. We stopped at the wharf. The children kicked pebbles into the brown water as Boyle waited in line to order food for us. Quinn stood next to me.

'I'm sorry about what I said last night. About birth. It was a stupid thing to say, considering what you and your wife went through.'

Without taking his gaze off the playing children, he replied, 'It was good to hear a happy ending. Or happy beginning, I should say. I wanted to apologise for being presumptuous.'

'Whatever do you mean?'

'I saw you yesterday with the children. You were dancing in the rain.'

I laughed. 'It was fun. We were covered in muck. Margery was a tad...discomfited. But why do you think you were presumptuous?'

'That evening at the cove, when you asked me my reason for staying away from you for three months. Do you remember what I said?'

'That we'd both lacked courage.'

'Yes. And that was presumptuous of me. I'm sorry I said that.'

'But your assessment was correct.'

He shook his head. 'I'm the coward, Elizabeth. You are the most courageous woman...no, *person*...I've ever met. The oysters are ready.' Abruptly, he walked away and helped Boyle distribute servings of hot oysters, white bread, and a delicious sauce I'd never tasted before.

WE CONTINUED our trip into Somerville. As we turned onto Middlesex Avenue, Mystic River peeked through the tall grass of the marshes. Arthur's spine snapped straight. He tapped at the window, mouthing words I could not decipher.

We stopped where the corpse was found. Quinn asked Arthur if he remembered which way the carriage had come. The boy pointed back toward Somerville.

'How long did you hang on to the back of the carriage?' Quinn asked.

Arthur shrugged, gazed at his palms, and rubbed them on his trousers.

'Until your hands hurt?'

Arthur nodded.

'Hum,' Quinn said, and asked us all to get back into the carriage. We rode through Somerville and into Cambridge, past the Alumni Hall of Harvard University. Briefly, I wondered if they'd ever let me in. Perhaps when I was eighty or ninety years old. Not that it mattered.

'Stop!' I called after we'd crossed the Charles River and were going down North Harvard Street. I bent closer to

Arthur, who'd gone strangely still on reaching the apex of the bridge. 'Have you been here before?'

Frowning, he chewed on his lower lip.

'Are you not sure?'

He waggled his head side to side.

'Not sure. All right. Shall we go back?'

Slowly, he shook his head no, then pointed ahead. There was hesitation in the gesture.

I knocked on the roof and said loudly, 'Keep going. If we don't find anything, we should go back.'

A light smack of reigns to the backs of the horses, and off we went.

Arthur didn't know we were heading to the orphanage. Quinn had asked me not to tell him. He wanted me to watch Arthur's reaction when we got close. We followed the Charles River into Brookline. As the railway came into view, Arthur made a strangled sound.

Boyle lifted his hand to knock against the roof, but I stopped him. Whatever Arthur feared was right ahead of us. Klara grasped his fingers and tugged. He didn't even seem to notice.

'The orphanage is just two or three hundred yards ahead of us,' Boyle said.

'Tell him.' I nodded in the direction of the driver's seat. 'Ask them to drive past quickly. I'll keep an eye on the children.'

The closer we got to the orphanage, the harder Arthur's small body trembled. His fists were kneading his lap, his teeth clenched so hard I could hear the enamel screech. I placed my hand over his. Klara patted his knee. None of it registered. His terrified eyes flickered from the road, to the railway, the river, and back.

He began howling as we passed a pasture with a small flock of sheep. A farmhouse came into view. Arthur dropped from his seat and scuttled underneath it, the noises he produced those of a creature in pain.

'Get the boy away from here!' I snapped. Boyle was already moving. He exited the carriage as Quinn jumped onto the street. Masters slapped the horses and they took off at a fast trot. I crouched down and tried to comfort Arthur. But he had his face tucked against his knees, refusing to look up. Not even his fingers were splayed against a firm surface. He was done communicating. The world was too terrifying, so he shut it out.

The carriage bounced over potholes and cobblestones. Arthur compacted himself into a ball. Only when Klara curled her small body against his, did the boy crack his eyes open.

'We drove away from that place,' I told him.

He squinted at my mouth. Then flung out an arm as far as the constricted space allowed.

'Yes, we are leaving. This orphanage... Was that your home?'

A nod. His lips pressed to a slash.

'But you were adopted a few months ago?'

His ribcage heaved. His eyes darted to the window, the door, to Klara.

I touched his hand. 'It's all right. You are safe now.'

That only seemed to terrify him more. He scrambled from his hiding place, took one look out the window, and yanked the door open. He was gone before Masters could stop the horses.

13

*A*rthur had leapt over a fence, and was racing across the sheep pasture we'd just passed. Screaming, Klara clung to my leg when I tried to make her to stay in the carriage with Masters. There was no time for discussion. With my daughter perched on my hip, I ran after Arthur, the sergeant right beside us.

'Please keep a few paces away, Sergeant Masters.' I lifted Klara over the fence, and put her up on my shoulders when I joined her on the other side. 'The boy is terrified of strangers.'

He grunted in the affirmative. Although his build was that of a runner, Masters clearly wasn't one. The first two hundred or so yards had him pumping like a locomotive. The terrain was flat and the grass short. I had a good view and could run full out as long as Klara held on tight. Near a grove, not far ahead of us, Arthur was slowing down. He seemed undecided for a moment, then took a turn toward the river and sped up.

'Stop! Will you—stop!' Masters bellowed.

'The boy is deaf.'

'Right—uh—sorry.' Every word seemed to pinch his airways.

Klara's hands slid over my eyes, and I moved them farther up, told her to grab my hair instead. The grass became taller and the *squish squish* of my boots warned me to place my feet with more care, else I'd fall into a mud puddle. But it was a rotten branch dropped from a tree some months before that nearly took me down. I stumbled to a halt by the riverbank. Klara didn't make a peep. Her hold on my hair was painful.

'You can let go, dear one. Arthur will be all right. I promise.'

The boy's boney frame was folded over, his arms stuck elbow-deep in the mud. His movements were frantic, half-mad.

Masters caught up with us, clapped his palms to his knees, breathing so hard it sounded as if he might retch. 'What's the boy digging up over there?'

Strange noises of muffled ache fell from Arthur's mouth as he tugged at a piece of dirty, torn fabric. With a sucking noise, he pulled it free, together with a lump and something that looked like hair.

I felt the blood drain from my skin. 'Klara, stay with Sergeant Masters for a moment. I need to talk to Arthur alone.'

I shifted her from my shoulders into my arms. But before I could set her down, she leapt from my hold and ran up to Arthur. The wind was tugging at thistledown hair that stuck out from under her hat. Arthur had lost his hat. His hair was wet, bristly; his eyes dark and hollow with pain. A snot bubble hung from his nose, too stubborn to pop. He was more ghost than child. A skeleton. I'll never forget the terror and determination that exuded from him, or the small hand that reached up to touch his cheek. The small voice that said, 'Mama said you will be all right.'

I'll never forget the doll-like body he'd ripped from the mud.

~

REINFORCEMENTS ARRIVED SWIFTLY. First came the Brookline Police Department, and later, officers from the Bureau of Criminal Investigation. A kind soul brought sandwiches and tea for the children, and even a blanket. One policeman offered a handful of candy. Arthur refused to move away from the grave until Professor Goodman arrived at the scene. He took one look at the boy clinging to my side, and one at little Klara, who slept in my arms, tucked halfway under my coat. Pushing up his hat, Goodman asked, 'Are you the young gentleman who led the police to the bodies?'

'He reads lips,' I said. I was done telling people what Arthur couldn't do.

Goodman went down on one knee, pressing his impeccable trousers into the mud. He smoothed his moustache, and said slowly, 'You are very brave. It's all right to rest now. You have done enough for today.'

Arthur shook his head.

'There's more you need to do?'

One nod. And then he pointed toward the grove.

Breath froze in my lungs. I hadn't even considered the possibility...

'More dead children?' Goodman asked.

Arthur pressed his lips together and nodded again.

My legs felt watery. I lifted my gaze to find Quinn. Policemen were on their knees, small shovels in hand, others standing next to them, holding open paper bags and boxes to receive evidence. Then I remembered Boyle telling me Quinn was rounding up the orphanage staff. Until Arthur had dug up the corpse of an infant, the staff had been considered a potential source of information.

No one had expected *this*.

'Will you show me?' I heard Goodman say.

Arthur grasped Goodman's hand, not because he seemed to need — or even expect — support, but to make sure the man followed. The medical examiner's eyes darted over his spectacles and met mine. The mischievous glint he kept burning behind his irises had entirely vanished.

Carefully, I adjusted Klara's sleeping form in my arms, and followed Arthur to the grove. The boy marked an area among the trees with a sheets of paper torn from Goodman's notepad, and skewered into the wet ground with sticks.

My stomach roiled when he set off once again, not back to the riverbank, but across the pasture and up to the farm house. I'd never been so glad for Klara's slumber as Arthur opened the door to a privy and pointed down the hole.

The stink of fermenting excrements was strong, but beneath it lingered a sweet and pungent note. Faint. But unmistakable to those familiar with the odours of human decomposition.

I touched Arthur's cheek that was wet with rain, mud, and snot. Goodman offered his large handkerchief. Mine was so drenched and full of dirt, I'd left it in the police carriage.

'Are there more?' he asked. He was good. Not the faintest cringe or hesitation. It needed to be done.

Arthur shook his head, and hung it low. He sniffed and tucked his hands under his armpits. The picture of utter exhaustion.

Softly, I bumped my hip to his side to get his attention. 'Let's go home.'

He looked puzzled for a moment, then shocked.

'Our home,' I hastened to add. 'You, Klara, and me. We

will go home. Take a hot bath. And then we will eat and read in bed.'

A tiny smile flickered across his face.

'Hold on to my raincoat. We'll find Quinn, and...' I trailed off as I spotted him crossing the courtyard with two officers in tow. His gun was drawn. Instinctively, I moved in front of Arthur, but the boy pushed around me. He wanted to see.

Needed to see.

I scanned the courtyard, the buildings for danger. A barn and a pigsty. The farmhouse. Deep tracks of four-wheeled carriages in the muck. Prints of hooves and booted feet. Farthest away from us, near the entrance to the main building, a group of people stood surrounded by police officers. Some were complaining, others were silent. The men were shackled. Most of the women wept. They were surely waiting for a prison cart.

I turned my attention back to Quinn. He had one hand on the door to the pigsty, the other clutched his revolver. For a heartbeat, he looked across the courtyard and right at me. He seemed to be wondering what we were doing there, why we hadn't gone back home yet. I could see words form in his mouth as the pigsty door slammed open, and a pitchfork was thrust at his chest.

14

*I*t happened so fast, I couldn't even cry out, 'No!' Couldn't even tighten my hold on Klara. Or think of pulling my gun. Or do any other thing but blink once and stop breathing.

In this one blink of my eyes, the tines of the pitchfork went through Quinn's raincoat. The screech of the fabric would forever be burned into my mind. The popping sound of a button. I must have imagined these noises, for I stood too far away to have heard them.

The tines cut clean through the oilcloth as Quinn's upper body reared back, and his free hand snapped forward. He grabbed the handle and yanked, hard. The man who'd thrust the weapon came flying out the door, and instantly received the butt of Quinn's revolver against his temple. He fell like a dead tree. Ramrod straight, he smacked into the muck.

Quinn handed the pitchfork to one of the policemen, took the manacles from the officer's belt, and shackled his attacker. He rolled him onto his back and checked his breathing. And only then did he look down at his own chest.

I sucked in air, tasting blood in my mouth. I'd bitten a small gouge into the inside of my cheek.

'Bloody hell, I've never seen anyone move that fast.'

I jumped at Goodman's voice. I'd completely forgotten his presence. I looked down at Arthur, worried he might mistrust us even more now that he'd seen Quinn take down a man. But Arthur's face glowed with admiration. He poked out his lower lip and gave a nod.

I looked up. Quinn was smiling at him.

Leisurely, Quinn strode up to where we stood. As though getting the sharp ends of a pitchfork thrust at his heart meant nothing to him. He frowned. 'You look like death.'

I thought I'd lost you, sat on my tongue. 'Are you injured?'

'No. He was too slow.

I reached out and picked at the rends in his raincoat.

'It can be fixed,' he said with a shrug.

So blasé. I wanted to punch him. 'Arthur showed us another two sites. The privy.' I pointed my chin. 'And the grove by the pasture. He marked the place.'

Quinn's face fell. 'More graves?'

'Yes. I need to get the children home now.'

'Sit for a moment. I'll get a police carriage for you. Those,' he made a gesture at the prisoners, 'can wait in the rain until tomorrow for all I care.'

He led us over to a bench by the barn. I was grateful for the respite. My arms were burning from carrying Klara's weight for so long. The moment I sat, she woke up and told me she needed to piddle. I took her around the building and helped her with her clothes. When we got back to the others, Quinn was speaking with Arthur. I was surprised the boy was tolerating Quinn's hand on his. There was such reverence in the child's gaze. I didn't want to imagine all the horrible things the pitchfork man might have done to the children in his care.

Briefly, Quinn looked up at me, then continued to talk to the boy. His words were as much for the benefit of me and Goodman, as for Arthur. He spoke about the children in the orphanage: that they were receiving medical care; that officers of Brookline Police Department had called in their wives, sisters, and mothers to help; that the children would be transferred to a hospital until they felt better; that a good orphanage would be found. And that he would personally make sure all the children were treated well.

'You saved many lives today,' he said and took off his hat, shook off the rain, and placed it on Arthur's wet head. 'I am very proud of you. But I need to ask one more thing of you. In two days, the photographs of each man and woman you see over there...' Quinn thrust his thumb over his shoulder toward the group of dishevelled staff. '...will be ready for you to look at. Do you understand?'

Solemnly, Arthur signalled *yes*.

'Good. All you need to do is point at each photograph, and tell us if that person hurt or killed any of the children.'

Arthur pointed at his eyes and thumbed his chest.

'You mean to say you're ready to do that?'

He shook his head, pointed at his eyes and thrust his fist toward the staff.

'You...want to see them in person? In the holding cells?'

Yes, signalled Arthur. *Yes!*

Astonished, Quinn sat back. 'Tomorrow morning, then?'

The boy gave Quinn a nod that made his hat tumble to the ground.

'Good.' Quinn put the hat back on Arthur's head, squeezed his shoulder, and stood. 'You will have questions. Draw them for me. As pictures.'

~

IT WAS past ten o'clock that night when Quinn showed up at our doorstep, drenched, dirty, and worn to the bone. A police carriage was waiting by our gate.

I bade him come inside, but he declined. 'I'm on my way home. I need to see my daughter.'

'Is she ill?'

He shook his head. 'I need to hug her. Make sure she's happy. I've seen too much suffering today. Professor Goodman wasn't able to tell me the exact number of bodies that were recovered today, but it must be dozens. Most are skeletons that are…what did he call it…'

'Disarticulated,' I provided.

'Yes. The small bones came apart at the joints. The river worked them free. Dogs and rodents dug them up. But the privy.' He rubbed a palm over his face. 'By the gods, the privy! Goodman said the freshest corpses showed clear signs of having been alive when they were thrown in. The infants we found…' His shoulders were trembling. He stared hard at our threshold, his chest heaving. 'And the ones that were still alive. Starving. Small children tied by their legs to a ring in the wall or to a heavy log. All of them covered in lice and sores and…' His voice failed.

I took a step closer and wrapped my arms around his waist, and put my head against his shoulder. Air struggled through his windpipe. His heart staggered in his chest.

'Breathe with me,' I whispered, remembering how he'd taught me to breathe again after the Railway Strangler had put his hands to my throat and thrown his whole weight against me. I had believed I would never draw another breath.

Quinn slipped an arm around my shoulder and groaned. After several heartbeats, he calmed.

'How is Arthur?' he murmured.

'Exhausted, but fine. He and Klara were playing and reading. They fell asleep on my bed an hour ago. I'll have to squeeze myself really thin tonight.' I stepped out of our embrace.

Quinn's eyes were shut. With effort, he opened them and looked at me. It was as if I could see into him. The darkness I found there felt like home.

'We need to take your statement,' he said. 'The prisoners are being kept isolated from each other. Prevents them from agreeing on a single version of events. But when Arthur comes to identify them tomorrow, we'll put them all in one cell together with a few plainclothes detectives. He'll be safe. Make sure he knows that. But don't tell him about the detectives. A judge will be present as well because the circumstances are unusual. The key witness being the ward of the detective leading the case.'

'Will that be a problem in the trial?'

'No. That's why the judge will be there. It also helps that Arthur lives with you, not me. Everyone agrees that I had very little opportunity and no motivation to influence him. I'll be back tomorrow at nine. Good night, Elizabeth. And…thank you.'

'For what?'

'The hug. I needed it.'

∿

'I DIDN'T TELL you last night, because I wasn't sure,' Quinn began, as we jostled over bumpy streets the following morning. He threw a sideways glance at Arthur and Klara, who were drawing faces on the foggy window of the police carriage. 'Whatever Charles Hartwell was investigating, it had nothing to do with the orphanage. Arthur was taken away from that orphanage four months ago, and there's no building in the area that's high enough for a fall to cause the severity of injuries seen on Hartwell's body. None of the orphanage's staff remember seeing a man looking like Hartwell. And none of the staff have seen Arthur in the last few months. Hartwell must have been killed elsewhere.'

'I'm pretty sure they are lying.'

'I'm pretty sure most of them are. But the matron asked for leniency in exchange for information.' Quinn brushed an index finger over his moustache. The corner of his mouth curled in wry amusement. 'I granted it, of course. She didn't insist on a written agreement, and I failed to point that out to her. Naturally, neither Boyle nor I can recall exactly what it was she asked for. Or if she asked for anything at all.'

'How very unfortunate for her.'

'Indeed. She gave us the names of several other men involved in this...business. A physician who gave out death certificates for infants who were seriously ill, malnourished, and mistreated. While they were still alive. He would post-date the certificates by at least half a year so the orphanage would continue to receive monthly allowances from the Boston Children's Services even after the children were killed.' He dropped his hands to his thighs. 'Do you know what she called it? The matron? *A humane end to the suffering of the little angels.* It took all of my control not to break her neck right then.'

A bitter tickle ran up my gullet. I couldn't suppress a snarl. 'Dumping sick babies in the privy and letting them drown in shit is *humane*?'

Klara looked up and I clapped my mouth shut.

'Who's that?' I pointed at the drawing on the window.

'Arthur,' she said, lifting her chin and squaring her shoulders.

'You have to put Quinn's big hat on him,' I suggested. At once, she went back to squeaking her index finger over the foggy pane.

Quinn put his mouth close to my ear and whispered, 'I rarely ever wish death on anyone, but now I find myself hoping desperately that judge and jury will find them all guilty and send them to the gallows. If they aren't hanged, I'm not sure I won't take matters into my own hands.'

'Why did they do it? Did the matron tell you?'

'Money. Like most orphanages, they have been financing themselves through governmental fees and private donations. Once a year, they opened the orphanage to benefactors. Made sure to polish the place and display only their healthiest wards. Made sure to invite inspectors from the Board of Health that day, and made excuses for any other day the Board might try to schedule.' Quinn unfurled his fists and flexed his fingers. 'I wonder if one or more inspectors knew about this, and hid it. Because this *couldn't* have gone unnoticed!'

'The inspectors the Board of Health sends to Wards Six and Seven don't give a damn about the people there. The Board intentionally prettifies their data on infant deaths.'

'But why?'

'Because there are too many. We would all look like monsters if we knew that thousands of children were dying in the slums every year while we go about our own lives, bickering about the weather. But what happened to the older children? There must have been older children in the orphanage. Arthur couldn't have been the only one.'

He took a shallow breath, grasped my hand, and whispered over the clatter of wheels, 'That was their main source of income. Children four years and older were sold to factories, workshops, and domestic services. The pretty ones, though...'

'Brothels.'

'Yes. Elizabeth, we've stumbled into a child slave market. I want to slap myself for...' He trailed off, burying his face in his hand.

I touched his wrist. 'For not seeing monsters when you asked the staff about a missing boy?'

He dropped his hand. His face had lost all colour. 'Yes. I was arrogant. I fancied myself a good lie detector. I saw no fear, no pretence in the headmaster's eyes when he told me that no child had gone missing in the past weeks. And so I didn't dig any deeper.' He turned his gaze to the window. 'When he telephoned me to tell me that he recalled a mute boy having been adopted a few months back, I didn't smell the deceit. He sounded like a concerned and kind man. I remember thinking that the children were lucky to have someone like him.'

'Why did the man come forward to tell you about Arthur? He had so much to hide. Why draw more attention to himself?'

'I can't be sure, but I think he believed himself a suspect in the killing of Hartwell. He wanted to draw the attention away from himself.'

'So he conjured up the name Tillmann. That whole story.'

Quinn dipped his head.

'Are you sure Arthur was sold four months ago?'

'It was in their books. They didn't even use the children's names. Arthur was *the mute boy*. All the others were numbers.'

We trundled to a halt at Pemberton Square. Quinn opened the door, stepped down, and lifted Klara onto the pavement. Arthur jumped out, stuffed his hands into his pockets, and straightened his back.

'Are you ready?' Quinn asked him.

Arthur grabbed Klara's hand, and marched toward the police station.

Sergeant Boyle received us in the lobby and sent a young constable to inform Judge Cornell that the witness had arrived. 'It will just be a minute,' he said, and showed us to a row of chairs.

As we waited, I wondered who'd had bought Arthur, and if was the same person who killed Hartwell. Did the people who had been buying children from the orphanage know about their mistreatment, about the killings?

How could they not?

It didn't take long for three men in tailored suits to appear. They were introduced as Judge Cornell, Magistrate Peabody, and Peabody's officer, Mr Richards. They must have been expecting an avalanche of newspaper articles on the orphan killings, or else they wouldn't have pulled themselves out of their comfortable offices to witness Arthur's statement.

Judge Cornell seemed pleasant enough, but the Magistrate stared down his nose and said in a voice too high for a man that size, 'This is a police station, not a public playground!'

Quinn emptied his expression and changed into the man he'd shown me when we first met. His cold, calculating side. Even his voice was void of emotion when he said, 'I am sure the last thing our witness expects is for us to play games with him. If, however, it becomes necessary to provide him with reassurance, I will turn this police station into a playground. Unless you have a better idea for gaining the trust of a small child, one who did his best to point us to a crime as atrocious as any of us have ever seen? No? Very good. Let us proceed, then.' As he turned his back on the magistrate, I knew he'd have to pay for that lack of respect. Silently, I applauded his move.

Quinn took the lead down a flight of stairs. Arthur braced himself and followed, Klara holding one of his hands and I the other. Magistrate Peabody, Mr Richards, and Judge Cornell trailed behind us, murmuring about an upcoming boxing match. Their conversation ceased when Quinn entered the dank corridor that led to the holding cells. I remembered the day Watchman Hooper had knocked me over the head, and dragged me down there.

Quinn stopped walking. I pushed Hooper from my mind, and the fact that we were standing in front of the very cell I'd woken up in.

'Stand,' Quinn snapped at the prisoners.

I recognised two police officers among the group of more than a dozen men and women. The plainclothes detectives were among the prisoners not only to keep them from communicating or attacking one another but also to serve as identification controls. I hoped Arthur would take his time and not point at any of the policemen, whether from nervousness or confusion. He was only about six years old, and much was being asked of him.

It would make this case so much more complicated if there should be no credible witness. The bodies and the dozens of small skeletons gave evidence of the cruelties committed. But bones couldn't tell us who had done the killing, who had aided in it, and who had known nothing about it.

The judge manoeuvred himself in front of Arthur and spoke, 'Do you recognise any of these men and women?'

Arthur didn't move.

'It's your beard,' I said. 'He can barely see your lips move. May I?'

'Perhaps Inspector McCurley would do us the favour,' he grumbled, and stepped aside.

Quinn went down on one knee. 'Do you know these people?'

Arthur nodded.

'I will ask them to step forward one by one. If that person mistreated you or any of the other children, you must nod or point. Later you draw for me what each one did. All right?'

Arthur signalled *yes*.

'Line up,' Quinn said to the prisoners. 'First man on the left, step forward.'

Arthur grasped Quinn's hand so hard his knuckles lost all colour. With the other hand, he pointed at the man, produced a nod and a dull sound in the back of his throat.

It went on. Quinn called forward each man and woman, one after the other. Arthur always both pointed and nodded to make sure we understood. Four times, he shook his head no. When it was done, the boy was pale and trembling, his hair plastered to his temples. Not only had he faced his nightmare, he had worked so hard to understand and be understood. Annie Lowell, Arthur's sign language tutor, had told Quinn and me that even the best lip readers could only make out half a person's words by lip reading. Everything else was interpretation of body language, gestures, expressions, and letting the mind fill the gaps. Lip reading was exhausting under the best circumstances, and Arthur hadn't had that luxury.

'You did very well,' Quinn told him. 'Did you see any of the prisoners bury a baby?'

A shudder went through Arthur. He jerked down his chin.

Quinn told all the people Arthur had identified to remain in line, and the others to sit down.

'Can you point at the ones you've seen do it? I promise they can't harm you.'

Arthur lifted a hand. And motioned at the entire row.

'All of them?'

Yes, he signalled.

'Did you see any of them kill the man you were found with?' Quinn had to slowly repeat his question twice for the boy to understand what he wanted.

Arthur's shoulder sagged. He shook his head. Quinn looked up at me and gave me a small nod. *As I thought*, his eyes said. He softened his expression and addressed the boy once more, 'Did you see how Charles Hartwell was killed?'

A nod.

'Do you see the person who did it in this cell?'

No, he signalled. *No.* Arthur twisted his neck to look at me and Klara, desperation carved into his face.

15

A few days of normalcy was all that I wanted for the children. The rain stopping, and a day at the market. An evening at the cove stomping about in our wellingtons, throwing stones and sticks into the surf, and feeding stale bread to the ever-hungry gulls. A few hours with Miss Lowell, learning sign language. And explaining to Arthur that this was his home now, as long as he wanted it.

He wanted it so much that he came to me every day to ask if he could really stay. He drew pictures of the house, the garden, the sea. Of Klara, Zach, Margery, and me. He would point at himself in those pictures, a question raising his eyebrows. And my answer was always the same.

This is your home.

Somehow, it felt like a lie. I couldn't guarantee anything. I was not an American citizen. If I tried to adopt Arthur, I would face a bureaucratic and legal marathon with little chance of success. Our solution was unconventional. Quinn had gone to the Probate Court to get the adoption papers. Arthur was now legally his, but the guardianship for the boy would be transferred to me.

I had laughed when he suggested it. Told him that our neighbours would throw a big social event just to tittle-tattle about the inspector and the woman physician with the impossible haircut raising a child together in two different homes.

He'd just smiled and said, 'It will be nice of us to provide a little entertainment for the old and feeble.'

STANDING AT THE BAY WINDOW, I unfolded Quinn's letter again. I'd read it once, this collection of hastily scribbled notes. He was throwing his raw thoughts at me, hypotheses, and bits of information, in the hope I would come up with ideas.

The matron had given the police a wealth of information: how long they'd been selling children (eight years), how many physicians were on their payroll (two), the names and addresses of the many people who'd bought the older children, the number of infants dumped at the orphanage's doorstep each year (three dozen, or thereabouts), but no estimation of how many children had died of malnutrition, starvation, sickness, or from suffocating in a hole in the ground. They'd not bothered to count them.

The exhumation had taken two full days. Goodman and his assistants had managed to reassemble the skeletons of thirty-six infants and children. Nine bodies were largely intact. Over two hundred other small bones lay scattered across several improvised tables in the morgue, waiting to be puzzled together.

Newspapermen kept clogging Pemberton Square, and wild theories were being thrown around by everyone and his dog about the boy who'd discovered the "River of Bones" as the site had come to be called.

I held up Quinn's letter and read again the last lines in the fading evening light.

THE MATRON REFUSES to talk about the people who took Arthur. Not one of the staff will say a word about the boy's "adoptive parents." Several of them admit to having played a part in the deaths of their wards. They do not hesitate to give the names of the other buyers (if able to recall them), but whenever I bring up Arthur's buyers, I hit a wall of silence.

I WENT to pick up Rosie's receiver, and asked to be connected to the Boston Police Department Headquarters. The sergeant at the front desk told me that Inspector McCurley wasn't in, but he'd leave a message to telephone back as soon as possible.

Which Quinn did the following day around noon, just after I'd returned from delivering a baby at Ward Six.

'Did you see my notes?' he asked. The connection was better than it had ever been. There was no need to yell to be understood. I almost found myself marvelling at the invention of the telephone.

'Yes. That's why I wanted to talk to you. Have you considered the possibility that Hartwell bought the boy?'

'Yes. But Hartwell's widow, his children, and the neighbours all said they'd never seen him with a boy fitting Arthur's description. If we can believe the orphanage's records, Arthur was sold six or seven weeks before Hartwell left to investigate his story. It might well be that Hartwell ran into Arthur during his investigation.'

'Hum. Have you found the other children who were sold?'

'Yes. I want to talk to you about that. And we still need

your statement. It's not urgent, but if you could come to Pemberton Square in the next two or three days?'

'What about this afternoon?'

'Just a minute.' There were some scratching and rustling noises. 'Yes, I should be back in my office by three o`clock, or thereabouts.'

'I'll…see you then.' I stared at the receiver that crackled and ticked, and then fell silent. 'Rosie, your social skills are lacking.'

I CALLED on Hattie to see how she and her twins were doing. But my mind and heart weren't in it. And she knew it.

'One might think you're about to fall asleep.' Grinning, she patted my cheek as if I were a child. 'Let's invite the Freaks for lunch.'

'No! You need your rest, and I have to go the police and give a witness statement.'

'When?'

'Three o'clock.'

'Pffft! That's in two hours.' She reached up and pulled the bell rope.

Her maid showed up within seconds and bobbed a curtsy. 'Ma'am?'

'Telephone my brother to get the Freaks over here. Quick, or they'll miss Liz again. And tell Cook to prepare lunch for six. You may leave now.'

'Did anyone ever tell you that you are dictatorial?' I asked her, wrapping the question in a smile, although it wasn't all joke. I wanted to go home, not socialise with friends who wouldn't understand why I hadn't been able to see them for months. Who wouldn't understand why I did what I needed to do: the slums; Arthur.

The wound the orphanage had left in him was festering, and I felt a constant pull toward home, to the children.

My children.

I brushed the feeling aside, knowing that neither Klara nor Arthur needed me clinging to them around the clock. They were probably helping Margery, playing in the house, or learning their letters and numbers.

I smiled. Miss Lowell was still shocked when she saw Klara — a three-year-old! — reading aloud to Arthur. And not just a children's picture book, but Knowles' *The Legends of King Arthur and his Knights*, a volume that was littered with sentences half a page long.

THE FREAKS ARRIVED within the hour. Half of them, anyway. The poor cooks had slaved in the kitchens to put together a five-course meal in record time. Uriel pressed a wordless kiss to my cheek. His haggard look pinched my heart.

Warren, on the other hand, beamed with mischief. The mighty black eye he was sporting was only enhancing that effect.

I snorted at him. 'You look very much like the day we first met.'

My friends stared at me as if I were mad. Hattie pointed a fork at my face and rolled her eyes. That's when I recalled the cut over my eyebrow. I'd received it that morning in Ward Six, and had already forgotten about it.

'She was knocked on the head by a drunkard,' she supplied.

I shrugged, and turned my attention back to Warren.

'No offering of medical skills?' He waggled his eyebrows.

I waggled mine back at him. 'Your nose doesn't seem broken this time. May I fix that for you?'

He burst out laughing, then copied Uriel and kissed me

on the cheek, letting his lips linger a moment longer than necessary.

I elbowed him away. 'Where are the other three?'

'Jerome is…hiding. Margaret and Eliza are still in bed. We had a long and exhausting night, the pretty ladies and I. That's where I got this delightful black eye, by the way.' He paused, eyebrows raised in expectation.

Seeing that none of us was falling for his innuendos, he continued, 'Performing with those two at the Howard Athenaeum is an adventure I don't recommend to anyone. Being the nice gentleman that I am, I only played the piano, but *they* riled up the masses, taking the piss out on gender roles. Cited that idiot Acton up and down, but reversing the sexes.'

Theatrically, he raked back his hair, batted his lashes, and spoke in a girlish voice, *'The best fathers, husbands, and managers of households know little or nothing of sexual indulgences. Love of home, children, and domestic duties are the only passions they feel. A modest man seldom desires any sexual gratification for himself. He submits to his wife, but only to please her.'* Warren cleared his throat, and held up a hand to count on his fingers. 'I was hit by a boot, an umbrella, and a suitcase that must have been filled with rocks and reserved for the sole purpose of knock out unsuspecting artists. Not to mention all the rotten vegetables that flew our way.'

'Are Margaret and Eliza injured?'

'Of course not! I jumped in front of the heavy missiles.' He waved his arms and threw out his chest until I guffawed. 'It's good to see you laugh, Liz. You look so sombre these days. Worse than Uriel, even. Why is that?'

I reached out to squeeze his hand. 'Not today, Warren.'

We ate and talked, skirting around all the heavy issues. A knot began to loosen in my chest and I realised that I'd needed this. A distraction from all the dark things going on in our lives. Before I left, I took Uriel aside to ask him about his friend. We all knew Jerome was in love with him.

'There is nothing I can do, Liz. He hates himself for it. He's disgusted by the thought of loving a man.' Scowling, Uriel lifted a shoulder. 'I love him as a friend but nothing more.'

'A tragic love story.'

'And there's another one playing out.' Uriel shifted his gaze to Warren and back at me.

'I am honest with him. That's all I can do. He has to figure out the rest.'

WHEN I ARRIVED BACK HOME, Zachary told me that Quinn had telephoned from the police station to cancel our meeting. Frowning at the floorboards with his arms akimbo, he added, 'Something's up. The way he spoke... Brief. Impersonal. It sounded the way you'd talk if people were listening in. You know what I mean?' He narrowed his dark brown eyes at me.

'He couldn't speak freely.'

Zach nodded.

'What precisely did he say?'

'He said his name. Very official-sounding. Inspector McCurley of the Bureau of Criminal Investigation. Said he required Dr Arlington to come in tomorrow morning to give a witness statement, and if she has any question he'd be available today until four in the afternoon.'

I picked up Rosie's receiver and asked the operator to connect me with Pemberton Square. It took several minutes to get Quinn on the telephone.

'Inspector McCurley of the Bureau of Criminal Investigation.' He knew it was me, yet he found it necessary to make an official introduction.

'Is it urgent?' I asked softly.

'Yes.'

'Say something about the witness statement tomorrow. What time you want to see me.'

'Would ten o'clock be convenient for you, Dr Arlington?' The distance in his voice made my stomach roil.

'Are you leaving your office at four?'

'Yes, that it quite right.'

'Do you want to come directly to Savin Hill?'

'My apologies, Dr Arlington, but that won't work.'

That left only one place. 'In two hours at your apartment?'

'I might be able to arrange that. Have a good day, Dr Arlington.' With that, he was gone. I clicked the receiver back onto its hook, and blinked at Zach who was leaning against the wall, arms crossed over his chest.

'Is it bad?' he asked.

I could only nod.

16

'*J*'m sorry I had to be such an arse on the telephone, but I couldn't risk... Who *did* this?' Quinn's voice had a sharp undertone as he touched his fingers to my brow. I watched his eyes as they sharpened on mine. The darkening of his irises as his pupils flared.

'I attended a birth this morning. Ward Six. A stone-drunk husband was attacking the furniture, his labouring wife, and me. As I was kicking him out I got lobbed on the head.' I tried a non-committal shrug.

Quinn motioned me inside. 'I can teach you how to defend yourself better.'

'Zach spars with me occasionally.'

'You'll learn more from me.'

We sat. He poured tea. Notes lay scatted on the table before us. He was still holding my gaze, waiting for an answer.

'No matter how excellent a pugilist I might become under your tutelage, I'd still get punched, because I'd not be focussed of winning a fight, but on helping a baby into the world or not botching a surgery.'

'I can show you how to knock them out in a blink.'

My eyebrows rose. 'Sober men get rather difficult when I ask them to punch me in the mouth.'

'I'll be asking *you* to punch *me* in the mouth.' Quinn laughed. 'I'll show you how to look for openings. Learn how to hit before you get hit. If you agree, we'll train every evening for two weeks. Once you know the basics, we'll adjust the schedule.'

'All...right.'

Now he was the one looking sceptical. 'Are you scared?'

I put a hand to my heart and lifted my eyebrows. 'Massively.'

Sniffling came from the bedroom, followed by a muffled cry. Quinn hurried to his daughter and carried her back into the sitting room. 'She's been running a fever since this morning. But I think it's going down now,' he said, as he touched his cheek to her forehead.

I reached over and put my fingers to the back of her neck. 'Does she have a rash? Any discolouration of her tongue? Diarrhoea?'

'No, just a fever. It might be a tooth coming in.' He gazed at his daughter, but it was obvious that his thoughts had strayed far away. 'The reason I called you...'

The temperature in the room dropped.

'I am not supposed to tell you this. Or, in fact, anyone. Earlier this month, the Chief Superintendent called all detectives in the Bureau of Criminal Investigation into his office. A man from the Secret Service was waiting for us. He told us that counterfeiters have been operating in Boston for four or five months, and they believe it's the Lancaster gang that they've been chasing for two years now. It turns out the Lancaster police botched the investigation, and the counterfeiters got away without even being identified. The time window fits. The quality of the counterfeit money that's been found here is similar to or even better than what was circulating in Lancaster. The Secret Service detective called it a conspiracy of a magnitude and danger unlike anything the Treasury Department had ever seen. And he asked that all our police officers report to him every single treasury note we find during raids. He said to look high-quality notes in gambling halls.'

'Did he say how the money was made?'

'They aren't sure. The only thing their experts can agree on is that the counterfeits must have been produced by a combination of photo-etching and hand engraving.'

Líadáin kicked out with a cry, but settled down quickly, thumb in mouth.

Quinn lowered his voice as he continued. 'Around noon today, an officer from the Medford Police delivered a package to me. He'd read about the killing of Charles Hartwell and connected it to a complaint a landlord filed. One of the tenants didn't pay the rent, never returned to his room and left everything untouched. As if—'

'...he fell off the face of the earth.'

Quinn nodded. 'The officer gave me a description of the man, based on the statement of the landlord. I telephoned the landlord for confirmation, and asked if a boy had been seen with the tenant.'

I was sitting at the edge of my seat, one knee digging into a table leg.

'He remembered Arthur very well.'

'Are you sure? Arthur tries hard not to be noticed.'

'I asked the landlord about that. He said his tenant, whom he knew by the name of Charles Smith, had insisted that the boy stay in his room until he returned. He didn't specify where he was going but said he'd be back the following day and wanted the boy to guard his belongings. An excuse to keep the boy safe, I'm sure. The landlord didn't like it and kicked Arthur out the moment Charles Hartwell left.'

I pressed the heels of my hands against my eyes but flinched back when I touched the cut on my brow. 'What precisely *is* the Secret Service? I read about them once in the papers. An article about counterfeit cigar labels, or some such.'

'They investigate fraud against the government, mostly. Counterfeit money, false identification papers, and the like. The Secret Service is an agency within the Treasury Department.'

'Their name makes them sound more like an espionage unit.' I shook my head. 'As much as I want to rail against that landlord, his unkindness turned out to be fortunate. If Arthur hadn't been kicked out, we wouldn't have found him. He'd probably still be...wherever he was. But what does Hartwell have to do with the Secret Service?'

Quinn placed a gentle hand on top of Líadáin's head, trailed fingers through her hair, and frowned. 'I found a counterfeit banknote in Hartwell's diary. The note was the only piece of hard evidence for what Hartwell was investigating. Connect that with the copper shavings found in Arthur's clothes: High-quality copper is used in printing plates. Unfortunately, all of Hartwell's notes are...diffuse. He never mentions names or locations.

He describes the movements of six men, calling them man A, man B, and so on. Building A and building B, workshops, warehouses. He writes about Arthur without identifying him. *A young fellow with remarkable abilities*, is how he describes him. If the boy is indeed Arthur. Hartwell never mentions his age or that he is mute.'

'What was Arthur doing for the counterfeiters? And why would Hartwell not be more specific in his own notes? Fear, certainly. But...of what or whom?'

Quinn's jaw ticked. 'In his final entry, Hartwell hints that someone in Boston's Police force is involved.'

'Bloody hell!'

'And that's why I didn't tell anyone about this. The Medford Police officer didn't bother to read the diary. And no one of the Boston Police force knows about this. Not the Chief. Not even Boyle. When you and I were supposed to meet for your witness statement, I was on my way to the Boston offices of the Secret Service. They asked me to work with them. I declined.'

'What? Wouldn't that solve all your financial problems? I'm sorry. None of my business.'

Quinn huffed a laugh. 'I didn't ask for extra payment. I asked for two small favours, but they wouldn't budge.

'What requests? If I may ask?'

'That you would be my consulting detective.'

Prickling ran down my spine. 'You are jesting. A woman on the police force?'

'Do you find it unusual that men in positions of power refuse to work with a woman?'

'No! It's the norm. But why refuse the offer? You want to solve this case. I know you do.'

Quinn lifted a shoulder. 'None of this would have come out, if not for you and Arthur. You should get credit for it. Or at least accept credit, if someone offers it to you.'

I leant back in my chair, nonplussed. 'But if I get used to recognition, I'll keep expecting it, which will inevitably lead to a lot of disappointment.'

'Expect it from me, then.'

'What was your other request?'

'That they do everything in their power to keep Arthur safe and in your home. He's been dragged around enough.'

'Why would they decline *that?* He's their only witness.'

'They don't think he'll be worth much on the witness

stand. The boy is only six years old, and can't even speak. The copper shavings might or might not connect him to the counterfeiters. And even if he'd been in their workshop, did he understand what they were doing?'

Leaning back and shutting his eyes, he grumbled, 'The Secret Service is trying a power grab. With this the biggest counterfeit case in history and with the current recession causing the banks to panic, they have the leverage to force our Chief Superintendent's hand. They've requested all our notes and reports, everything we have on the Hartwell murder. We've been taken off the case, effective today. The Secret Service doesn't much care whether I work with them or not. The snobs don't believe they need the boy either…'

He stopped, blinked, and shifted his gaze to me. 'I wonder if they are waiting for the counterfeiters to try and silence Arthur? Damn it to hell and back! As soon as the counterfeiters' man in the Boston police department puts two and two together, Arthur won't be safe.'

'Are you sure they have someone? Wouldn't that man have recognised Arthur when he was brought to Headquarters?'

'Their man isn't necessarily stationed at Headquarters. And I doubt he's ever seen the boy. That would have required the counterfeiters to absolutely trust a policeman, enough to invite him to one of their hideouts and let him see the faces of their men. That's extremely unlikely. They will have used one man, or two at the most, to exchange information for payment.'

'What will they do next? The Secret Service I mean.'

'They'll raid all the workshops and warehouses in Medford tonight.'

'How…subtle.'

He snorted.

I chewed on the inside of my cheek. 'Zach and I are

keeping Klara safe at all times. We can protect Arthur as well. But those raids will alert the counterfeiters that someone's leaked information. They will suspect the orphanage staff. The gang knew when Arthur disappeared and Hartwell's body was discovered. They must know about the raid on the orphanage by now. If they have any brains, they'll have packed and left. I doubt they'll bother coming back for Arthur. He's mute, and only six years old. He doesn't have much value for them. He might have just been sweeping the workshop floors, for all we know. And I doubt they see him as a big enough threat to be worth getting him out of the way. The risk of discovery is too high.'

Frowning, Quinn nodded once.

My gaze drifted from his face down to little Líadáin, slumbering red-cheeked and feverish in his arms. 'How is her temperature?'

He touched her forehead, her neck. 'It's nearly gone.' His soft smile sent my heart knocking against my ribs.

He stood, and walked to his bedroom. I'm not sure what it was that compelled me to follow, but the thought of staying behind put my stomach in knots.

I watched him carry his daughter to bed and tuck her in. At the quiet snick of the door against its frame, he looked up. Slowly, his spine straightened. The heavy blue of his irises was swallowed by the black of his pupils.

Only then did I realise that I'd closed the door behind me.

I'd shut us into in his bedroom.

17

*H*e approached. Slowly. His brow in furrows, eyes hooded. He came to a halt only inches from me, holding my gaze with his own.

He raised a hand and gently touched my bruised eye. His other hand was curled to a fist by his side, as though he was unsure whether I would allow him to touch me. Perhaps he wondered if he should allow himself to touch me. A low growl vibrated in his chest as he took the final step closer.

A thunderstorm rolled beneath my skin when the heat of his body hit mine. His fingertips brushed over my cheekbone, my temple. His gaze was intent, but guarded.

I placed my hand on his chest. He froze, waiting to be pushed away.

I rested my palm there. Softly. Over his heart, feeling the rumble.

His hand on the side of my face twitched, nearly contracted. Then he traced his thumb along my eyebrow, careful of the bruising, and down, down along the line of my jaw to my chin. His breath a battle, his gaze on my lips, he paused.

I reached up, and explored his face the way he'd explored mine. Slow. Considerate. And still, he waited. Observed. When my fingers touched his lower lip, he leant into me, and brushed a kiss to my eye. I flinched as his moustache prickled the swollen cut on my brow.

He pulled back, said, 'Don't leave,' and stepped away.

I felt like falling.

He unbuttoned his shirt and dropped it over a screen by a small washbasin. The tail of a serpent curled around the biceps of his left arm, continued up his shoulder and down his spine to disappear around his waist. I yearned to see the entire tattoo, but my feet wouldn't move an inch.

He drew water from the tap, picked up soap and a shaving brush, and worked a lather onto his moustache, his chin and cheeks. A small lamp threw soft light across his back. Muscles rolled beneath skin in unhurried movements. I imagined the black scales of the serpent rippling in the light. With calculated strokes, he took off the moustache and shaved his jaw. He splashed water on his face, then rubbed it off, and threw a brief glance in the mirror at his now-naked face, the slightly paler skin above his upper lip.

When he reached for his shirt, I said, 'Don't.'

A moment's hesitation, then he pulled it over his shoulders and slowly buttoned it, hiding the serpent's massive head behind a layer of white cotton. When he stood before me, he said, 'Just so you know you can change your mind any time.'

'Do you know me to be a fickle woman?'

A smile lifted the corner of his mouth. 'No, but I know you as a scientist. You haven't gathered data on my kissing skills yet. They might make you want to run away.'

I huffed, and he continued his silent exploration of my face, one hand again curled to a fist by his side as though to hold on to himself, the other outlining my features.

His eyes fell shut as I leant into his palm.

I brought my lips close to his, feeling his breath feather across my mouth. I flicked out the tip of my tongue. Groaning, he took my hand and pressed it over his heart.

'Are you done wearing this shirt yet?' I asked.

His eyes snapped open, irises black with longing. 'You may do with it as you wish,' he said hoarsely.

I lifted an eyebrow at him, then opened the three top buttons, pausing to slip my fingers around his throat. 'When I first met you, I wanted to wrap my hands around your throat, and shake you.' I dipped my head and kissed the small divot where his collar bones met.

He inhaled sharply.

I undid the next button and the next, until his breastbone was bared. The serpent stared at me, its forked tongue dashing out of a fanged mouth. 'When I met you the second time, I wanted to strike you right here. To cut off your air so you would stop your barking.'

'I never bark.'

'To me, it sounded a lot like barking.' When all the buttons were freed, I splayed my hands over his abdomen. 'Strange. I can't seem to remember what I wanted to do to you the third time we met.'

'You threatened to throw a clyster at my head.'

I laughed. 'Did I? Oh, yes, I remember.'

Silence fell. My fingers followed the coiled body of the snake from waist to chest. Where my hand touched his skin, his muscles tensed.

He whispered, 'And the first time you wanted to kiss me?'

'Do you want me to skip over all those times when I felt the urge to shoot a hole through your ball sack?'

A snort burst from him. 'I admire your violent tendencies, Dr Arlington.' He dipped his head, his lips a hairbreadth from mine. 'Tell me. When was the first time you wanted to put your endearing mouth to mine?'

A dark, deep noise rumbled up my throat. 'It happened slowly. Gradually, I think… Perhaps the day you told me why you named your daughter Líadáin.'

He pulled back. 'You wanted to kiss me because you pitied me?'

I curled my fingers around his waistband to keep him close. I couldn't bear the thought of him stepping away from me. 'No. I admired your strength. And I admire it more every day.'

He relaxed, cupping my face. 'And now? Why do you want to kiss me now?'

'Because…' I placed my palm over the scar at the side of his face, tracing his eyes, nose, and lips — those mesmerising, stubborn lips — with my gaze. 'Because the more you allowed me to see of you, the more I liked what I saw.'

He dug his fingers through my hair, his gaze that of a bird of prey ready to pounce. 'And now that you have seen all of me?'

'Have I?' I ran my hands around his waist, and up, up his spine, to his neck, trapping him in the circle of my arms.

Our mouths met in a sweet and awkward collision, unused to this intimate dance of lips and tongues. Fingers hurried over skin and found a rhythm. He whispered my name against my lips. As I sighed into his mouth, a trembling racked his body. His need matched mine, and only then did I realise how much I had missed intimacy. The meeting of two minds, bodies, and souls. For years I hadn't been touched the way he touched me right then. Not since I left Garret to hide in the Sussex Downs. And certainly not when I was abducted and forced into marriage with James Moriarty.

My body stilled. My lips froze on his. Slowly, I pulled back.

Quinn's dazed gaze sharpened at once. 'It's like the tide is going out. Why? What did I do?'

I reached out to touch his chest. 'There's so much about me you don't know.'

'And there's a lot you don't know about me.' He waited.

I inhaled and made myself say, 'You'd hate me if I told you everything…about my past.'

'Shouldn't I be the judge of that?' He placed his hand over mine. 'But I understand your concern.'

'You do?' I grew cold with foreboding.

His face fell. 'You think I've gone behind your back to find out what you did in London or Berlin?'

'Well, I…'

'I'd never do that.' What dropped from his mouth was more growl than words. 'Not since… Not since I've come to know you better. But what I meant to say about under-standing your concern was… It was about me. Since you came into my life, I can't help wondering what you saw in me. Or if you even bothered to look.'

'I don't…understand.'

He touched his fingers to my cheek. 'Look at you. You are intelligent, educated, determined. You are passionate and empathic. A fascinating and beautiful woman inside and out.'

'You are drunk.'

'It's my opinion. Am I not entitled to it? And yes, I'm a little drunk on kissing.' For a brief moment, he smiled. 'I'm a gutter rat who became a detective by sheer luck. I learned to read and write at fifteen. Or sixteen. I'm not sure how old I am, whether my mother was a whore, or my father a drunken thief. I have no education but the little I've managed to scrape together over the years. I earn a pittance, and I live in a shabby apartment. There's no reason for you to want me.' It wasn't a question. Just simple observation. 'Given my past, you should know that…whatever it is you're afraid to tell me, whatever deed you believe will shock me, I have most likely seen it, and worse. Or even done it.'

I turned my face into his palm, and muttered, 'If you had, you would have swung for it.' Clearing my throat, I stepped back. He knew I'd killed my husband, but there was so much more. Cruelties. Failures. More death and suffering.

'Only if I'd been caught.' A mere whisper. He took a step toward me until his chest touched mine, my back flush against the door. 'We both need time to learn to trust again. I can't help but think I might destroy you, make you want to kill yourself. And you can't help but think… What is it that you think? That I would arrest you?'

'That you…would despise me.'

He shook his head. 'No. I don't believe that would ever happen. Give us time, Elizabeth.'

I slid an arm around his waist and nestled my face in the crook of his neck. He was just the right height to fit my head comfortably against his shoulder.

He pressed a kiss to my temple, wrapped his arms around me, and said softly, 'You need to know that…that I loved my sisters and my brother. That I love Líadáin so much it hurts. But I never knew how to love my wife. That is who I am.'

'I lived the life of a man for years. With all the freedom granted to men. I don't fit into a female mould, and won't let myself be forced into one. This is who I am.' The last bit came out sharper than intended. A warning.

'I wouldn't want you any other way.' Sighing, he raked his finger through my hair. 'I am not whole, Elizabeth. I will have to put myself back together before I can be good company for you.'

I turned my face up to his. 'I enjoy your company very much. And what better father could Líadáin ever hope for?'

'One who kept her mother alive.' He extracted himself from our embrace.

Anger and sadness rolled through me. 'All right. Let's do this your way. You could have kept her safe. All you would have had to do was supervise her every minute, and immobilise her whenever she became suicidal. Either with drugs or by tying her down. That's doable. I don't know who would have raised Líadáin and kept her safe from her mother, but if you had invested every minute of your life, every bit of energy you had, she might still be alive. So why didn't you?'

His nostrils flared. 'Because I couldn't.'

'Why?'

He balled his fists. 'I chose not to.' He turned away then, and sat on the bed, his gaze hefted onto his sleeping daughter. 'There were days I wished Ailis dead. I always had a choice. And I decided I couldn't be bothered.'

'Don't you see that you ask the impossible of yourself? Why are you judging yourself so harshly?'

He didn't answer.

'How long was she suicidal?'

There was a long pause before he said, 'As long as I knew her.'

My heart bled for him. 'Why did you two marry?'

'To make it better. No... No, that's not entirely true. Neither of us knew what it meant to love, what marriage and having children meant. We both thought we would be better off together than alone. That, somehow, the other could make us feel whole.'

My stomach clenched, my eyes burned. 'I am so, so sorry what Ailis's death did to you and Líadáin. But how—'

'You are crying,' he said softly.

I dashed the wetness from my cheeks. 'How is it possible that you went through this hell, and didn't lose your kindness?' I sank down next to him and slipped my hand into his. 'Quinn, I know I wasn't there. I didn't witness the things you could or couldn't do for her. I didn't witness her illness. How she made life unbearable for herself and for you.'

A shudder went through him.

Quietly, I continued, 'But I know that no one wishes to be drugged or shackled to a bed for years, just to be kept alive. I know that I would rather die.'

He sucked in a sharp breath.

I entwined my fingers with his. 'And I know *you*. I know what's in your heart. It's not possible that you are guilty of all the things you blame yourself for. It is *impossible*. You are warm-hearted and kind. You love your daughter. You saved her life, with no chance to save your wife in that same breath. You were faced with a decision that would have broken any other person. I know you need time to come to terms with… with being with a woman again. I need that time, too. I've never given my heart away lightly. And during those months in captivity, I…made sure to tuck it away. You and I have been hurt. It takes time to…allow ourselves to be vulnerable again.'

He dipped his nose against my head and brushed a kiss to my hair. 'You hold my heart already. It's terrifying. I keep expecting it to weigh you down. To break you.'

'I am very hard to break.'

'I know. That's why I—' He cut himself off with a shake of his head.

'Aren't we two utterly overcomplicated creatures?' I said half-jokingly. 'One small kiss and each of us feels compelled to give a speech on how little we are good for one another.'

'*Small* kiss?'

'Medium-sized, perhaps?'

'That sounds too much like *average*.' He placed a finger under my chin and lifted my lips to his for the briefest of moments. 'That was a small kiss. And our first kiss was a… first kiss. I certainly wouldn't call it small or average. Bigger than our second kiss, though. If you wish, you may extrapolate from that.'

'Two measurements are altogether insufficient for extrapolation.'

'They make a straight line.'

I snorted. 'Straight lines are suspic—'

His mouth on mine cut me off.

18

The sun had just begun to peek over a cloud-encrusted horizon when I tapped Arthur's shoulder. The boy jerked awake as if I'd slapped him. Holding up my hands in a peace gesture, I sat back.

He blinked sleep from his eyes.

'Everything is fine,' I assured him. 'I'm meeting with Inspector McCurley in three hours and I wanted to ask you something before I go.'

He followed me to the kitchen where I handed him a cup of milk. 'Do you like Zachary's workshop?'

He squinted at my mouth, then shifted his gaze up to my eyes and dipped his head.

'Let's go then. No, take your milk with you. Look, I have my coffee.' We made our way across the porch and through the wet grass. I unlocked the door to Zach's workshop and hit the light switch.

Sipping my coffee, I pulled up a rickety stool and waited until Arthur turned his attention to me. 'Did you work in such a place when your friend Charles Hartwell found you?'

He licked his milk moustache and nodded.

'How many men worked there?'

He held up both hands, showing six fingers. A short moment later, a seventh.

'Seven men. The tools they were using, do you see them in here?'

He waved his hands in front of his chest and pointed at me.

'I don't understand. You want me to fetch the tools?'

No! he signalled, lifted his hands again and showed me six fingers. Then he pointed at me and lifted the seventh finger.

'Oh! Six men and one woman?'

Smiling, he patted my arm and gave me a nod. I chuckled. 'How old were they?'

Arthur lifted his shoulders, then made a grand gesture with both arms. *Old.*

'How old am I?'

Old.

I burst out laughing. 'Finish your milk, young man. You need to grow strong bones so you can get as old as me.'

Obediently, he slurped his cup empty. I indicated Zach's workbench. 'The tools they used. Show me which ones.'

Arthur swivelled his head around and frowned. Then he started digging through toolboxes and shelves while I emptied the dregs of my coffee. He returned with an awl, a flat piece of rusty iron, a pipe, and the cloth Zach used to oil and clean my bicycle. After placing it all on the floor, he snatched up an oilcan, then pointed at the pile of things and produced a scowl.

'Are you missing something?'

More scowling and a nod.

'I might understand if you show me what they did with these things,' I suggested.

He flopped to the ground, positioned the piece of iron at his knees, and began scratching small swirls into the layer of

163

rust. I had a good idea where this was going, but I waited and observed.

I had to be sure.

He worked for several minutes, but didn't seem to be happy with himself. The awl hovered over the iron more often than it was used to scratch patters into it. I tapped my fingers against the floor in front of him to draw his eyes to my face. 'It does not need to be perfect. An outline is enough.'

His eyebrows went hiding behind his bangs. He gazed down at the sheet of metal and quickly scratched four lines into it. A rectangle. Then an oval in its centre, the number fifty inside of the oval and at the top corners of the rectangle. Ornamental squiggles all around the rectangle and a few scrambled letters below and above the oval. And then, with utmost care, Arthur wrote a sweeping signature at the bottom, and next to that, another.

I had to force my heart to cease the nervous hollering.

'They were making money?' I asked cautiously.

Arthur's brilliant smile lit up the entire workshop. Thoroughly proud of himself, he tapped the awl's pointy end against both signatures, and the handle against his chest.

'You engraved the signatures, and someone else engraved all the rest?' I had to repeat myself, but as soon as he understood my question, he held up two fingers and nodded wildly. Finally, someone understood!

'You and two men did the engraving?'

He dipped his head.

'Were you well liked?'

He squinted at my mouth.

'The men like you and the work you did for them?' I repeated.

One big nod and a smile.

'Will they miss you?'

He waggled his head and shrugged. *Maybe, maybe not.*

I was sure they'd miss him. Recalling the calluses on his elbows and knees, I asked, 'You worked like this? On your elbows and knees?'

He nodded, grabbed the metal plate, dribbled oil onto it, and wiped the oil carefully into the scratches with the cloth. Then he knocked the plate flat against the floorboards, and picked up a piece of scrap paper to rub it vigorously over the plate. He flipped the plate around and pressed it against another piece of crumpled paper, using the length of pipe as a rolling pin.

I inhaled a long, slow breath and blew it out. 'Arthur, listen to me carefully.'

~

To clear my mind, I took a detour through the Public Garden. Slowing my bicycle, I sorted through the little I'd learned.

Not only had Arthur worked four months with notorious counterfeiters and murderers, he'd forged signatures on treasury notes for them. He knew the faces of every single man and the one woman, had been able to describe them to me in detail, and reproduced the signatures of four of them.

To the counterfeit gang, he was both a great risk and valuable asset. So why had no one tried to take him away? Or even to silence him. If they were afraid the boy would give them away, why hadn't they acted already? They had not hesitated to throw an investigative journalist off a building, and I was sure they would do the same to Arthur if they thought him a danger.

Perhaps trying to find another forger and a safe location far from Boston was their first priority. But for me to hope they would underestimate Arthur's memory and communication skills would be naive and stupid. Even though there seemed to be no other explanation for the counterfeiters' silence.

I wondered why they had bought Arthur in the first place, whether the orphanage staff had known about the boy's unusual talent. The staff's silence spoke volumes. They knew who'd bought Arthur, and that the gang had a policeman on its payroll. Under those circumstances, I wouldn't have said a word either.

But where to turn for help?

The Secret Service hadn't been able to identify any of the gang members even after two years of investigation. If I should make an official statement in Arthur's stead to them, it probably wouldn't take long for that news to reach the Boston police and the counterfeiter's police operative. For the same reason, I couldn't go to the police either.

And Quinn... Quinn *was* a policeman, but also a friend. And more. Yet, I wasn't sure if I should tell him. It wasn't a matter of mistrust. He was protective of Arthur, and I was sure he'd help me find a way to anonymously feed every shred of Arthur's knowledge to the Secret Service, while somehow making sure they didn't leak it back to the Boston Police Department and the counterfeiters' agent.

But what would that cost him? Quinn would be involved in spoliation of evidence on a major crime. By asking him for help, I'd force him to decide between me and the law — his job.

No, I couldn't do that to him.

I KNEW I WOULD LIE, but during those minutes it took me to chain my bicycle to a lamp post at Pemberton Square and walk up to Quinn's office to knock at his door, I worked to convince myself that everything I was about to say would be honest-to-god. *It's all true. I would never withhold or manipulate evidence. I am a law-abiding resident.*

Lies are told best when the liar believes her own words.

When Quinn beckoned me in with a polite but distant, 'Good day, Dr Arlington,' I knew something was wrong. When he stepped aside to let me in, I knew what was setting my teeth on edge. And it only hardened my resolve.

'Detective Raymond, Secret Service.' A tall man in his thirties stood and held out his hand. I shook it. We all took our seats. Quinn threw me an apologetic glance when Detective Raymond wasn't looking.

'Before you give your witness statement to Inspector McCurley, I'd like to ask you a few questions.'

Raymond began to leaf through a folder, and spoke without sparing me a glance, 'You don't look like someone with three million dollars in gold in the bank.'

In my periphery, I saw Quinn freeze. I kept my eyes on Raymond until he deemed it necessary to look up. 'You have no response, Dr Arlington?'

'Where you expecting one?'

Sighing, he leant back, and plastered an expression of great pity onto his visage. 'Serious allegations have been made against you. A Board of Health Inspector reported you to the police for using unnecessary force on a man in Ward Six. Furthermore, one Mrs Haywood is accusing you of killing her husband and manipulating evidence in a serial murder case. I am aware that not all of these allegations might hold up in court. However...' He paused for dramatic effect, and tapped a pencil against his folder. 'Inspector McCurley witnessed you killing a suspect before you even knew that man's identity. Furthermore, the Inspector ran a background check on you and was unable find anything. It appears that...you don't exist.'

Some weird part of me was waiting for him to say *furthermore* again.

But he only shook his head sadly. In his eyes, I was a child that needed reprimanding. 'Would you care to answer?'

'I would, if I knew what it is you want of me.'

He placed the pencil aside and folded his hands on the desk. 'Dr Arlington, allow me to speak frankly. I have gotten the very strong impression that you are a foreigner who sneaked into the US using a false identity. Furthermore, bodies turn up wherever you go. You are witness to a most horrifyingly wicked crime, and you are about to give your statement, but I can't help but wonder how much truth is to be found in anything you might say.'

'Lucky for me there were more than a dozen police officers around who can confirm my account.'

He leant back and smiled. I wondered if I should do him a favour and appear cowed. 'You are dancing around the real issue, Detective…' I swirled a hand in the air as if to help my mind catch his elusive name.

'Raymond.' His expression soured.

'Yes, thank you. I doubt you are here to tell Inspector McCurley how to do his job. So what is it that I can help you with?'

Eyes hard, his mouth pressed to a thin red scratch, he bent forward. 'I need the name of the man who forged the papers you used to enter the United States.'

'What makes you think they are forged?'

'As I said, Inspector McCurley—'

'Investigated my past,' I cut him off. 'Before he could find anything of importance, the Boston Police Department received a missive from the Crown asking him to refrain from digging any further.'

At that, Raymond's jaw loosened around the hinges. He shifted in his chair and asked Quinn if that was true.

'It is as Dr Arlington said,' Quinn answered.

'Are you working for the British government?' Raymond enquired, his voice crisp.

I burst out laughing. 'As a *woman* spy, perhaps? Or a woman diplomat? There aren't even... I don't even know what one would call a female police officer. Woman police-man? *Policewoman?*'

Detective Raymond's moustache curled in distaste. 'No, that would be absurd.'

'I'm not allowed to reveal any details, other than I am a witness the British government wishes to protect. Inspector McCurley's investigations threatened my safety, and he was asked to stop.'

'And what precisely did you witness?'

'As I said, I am not allowed to discuss it.' I put my most polite expression onto my face. 'I hope that answers all your questions.'

Damn it to hell and back if Raymond's grin wasn't devil-ish. 'Not quite. I want you to tell me everything you know about the circumstances that led to the death of Charles Hartwell.'

'I take it you've read the postmortem report?'

He inclined his head a fraction, as though a full nod was too much to ask for.

'Then you know as much as I do.'

'I doubt that.' A tight smile, and then he made me repeat every detail the medical examiners and the microscopist had written in their reports.

After nearly an hour of that circus, he pushed a box across the desk, and lifted the lid. 'Do you know any of these people? Go ahead and look at them.'

My fingers sorted through dozens of photographs. Two and a half by four inches. Mounted on thick paper. 'Who are they?'

'Forgers and counterfeiters the Secret Service has apprehended in the past three years.'

I placed the photographs back into the box and pushed it toward Detective Raymond. 'I've never seen any of them.'

'May I ask where all your money comes from?'

'My late husband.' Still, I wouldn't look at Quinn, wouldn't even wonder what might be going through his mind right then.

'Yet another body. I see.'

I didn't bother to reply.

Detective Raymond leant back and folded his hands over his waistcoat. With a steely gaze, he tried to get on my nerves, to make me say or do something stupid.

I imagined him in his office, complaining about a paper cut.

Slowly, he nodded, as though I'd given away a great secret. 'You'll understand that we have to question the boy at length.'

'Of course. Do you wish to talk to him today?' After Arthur had engraved the rusty metal plate, I'd warned him to lie whenever anyone asked him about the counterfeiters. He'd swept the workshop for the men. They looked just like other grownups. Old. Forgettable. They'd made a fuss about printing pictures on paper. What was it precisely? He didn't know.

Arthur had caught on immediately. He was bright and sharp, that one.

'After you give your witness statement to Inspector McCurley. What was it about again? Infanticides?'

Ah, now he was trying to appear dumb and uninformed. Perhaps to give me a false feeling of safety? I didn't know and didn't care. 'I'm at your disposal, Detective Raymond.'

He pushed himself up. 'I'll see you later, Dr Arlington. Inspector, I appreciate your lending me your chair.'

The door shut. Quinn rubbed a hand over his face. 'I'm sorry about that. I would have warned you, but he walked in unannounced just before you were due.'

I nodded once, pulling my thoughts and emotions together.

'You don't believe me.'

'I believe you.' Blowing out a breath, I leant back and squeezed my eyes shut. 'Did he say anything about the raid?'

'They found a workshop and a warehouse, both empty but for a scrap of fraudulent paper.'

'Yes, I noticed he wasn't happy.'

Quinn snorted. 'That you can say.'

Silence fell between us. I saw the questions burning on his tongue. *Three million dollars? What did your husband do? What have you done? Why is the Crown interested in you?*

But what he said was, 'I'll soon have to call in Boyle and a stenographer to witness and record your statement.' He waited for me to say something. Anything. But I found myself unable to lie to him.

He said, 'Professor Goodman asked for you. He wants your opinion on peculiar marks he found on some of the bones. He also spoke about deformations. And I'd like you to talk to some of the older children. We've located most of them, and with the help of the Children's Service we're moving them to the Baldwin Place Mission. I'm sure Arthur would like to see them, too.'

'I'll think about it.' It would be good for the boy to have more closure. To see that the others were safe, thanks to him.

'What happened?' Quinn asked softly.

Those two words nearly tore down my resolve. I pulled in a breath and opened my mouth. Before the wrong words could spill out, I said, 'The case is solved, is it not? You have dozens of witnesses and suspects. An entire morgue full of evidence. You don't need my help anymore. And Arthur should be left out of this as much as he can be. It's time for him to enjoy his childhood.'

So far, no lies. Only omissions. I should have been proud of myself, but I wasn't.

Quinn made an effort to keep the confusion off his face. 'You are right.' He touched his upper lip where his moustache used to be. The memory of our first kiss shot a bolt of heat through my core.

'If you are having regrets, Elizabeth, please don't think I would hold it against you.'

Surprised, I blinked. I hadn't even considered he'd suspect *that*. 'I don't regret our kiss.'

'But?'

I shook my head. My mouth wouldn't form the lies I'd put on my tongue before entering his office.

'You haven't stopped dodging questions since the moment Detective Raymond...' He stopped himself. Tipped his head to the side. His eyes darkened. 'What are you hiding?'

I wished I could have explained myself right then. But that would mean putting Quinn's career on the line. If the Secret Service suspected that Quinn had withheld evidence on the biggest counterfeit case in history, they'd make sure he fell hard. He was already hiding a murky past. This would do him in.

Silently, I watched how his jaw worked and his gaze flattened. How mistrust seeped in. He knew I was withholding information.

'Don't do this.' His voice was a rasp of metal against stone.

The pain in my heart was acute when I made myself say, 'I'm sorry.'

— END —

❧

Dr Elizabeth Arlington and Inspector McCurley will return soon.

For sneak previews, frequent giveaways, and much more, join us at:
www.kickassheroines.com

Find my books here:
www.anneliewendeberg.com

AFTERWORD

·

A note on the counterfeit case: You probably hate me a little for ending this book on a cliffhanger.

When I neared the final chapter of *River of Bones*, I realised that the counterfeit case and the part Quinn has to play in it has grown a lot bigger than I had planned. It didn't feel right to squeeze it into this story. So instead, I'll give this case a book of its own.

I know, I know. It can be quite annoying that Anna Kronberg / Elizabeth Arlington rarely solves **all** the crimes in one go. Why doesn't she?

Thing is, I have an allergy to the "murderer was caught in mere days because our sexy detective duo has superpowers" phenomenon in mystery fiction. It's utterly unrealistic to let Liz and Quinn catch all the bad guys in a few days, while an expert unit has not been successful in two years. Sure, I could have written the Secret Service detectives as dumb as mushrooms, and let Liz and Quinn haul in the counterfeit gang with a mere flick of their fingers. But where's the fun in that?.

To me, a good mystery is not necessarily to arrive at the

end — the solving of the case — but to be part of the dance of law enforcement and crime.

A note on lip reading: I hope my deaf readers will forgive that Arthur seems unusually apt at lip reading. He's such an integral part of this story, yet I rarely point out how hard it is for him to communicate with the hearing people around him (and Arthur doesn't even know sign language yet).

I did this for two reasons. First, the story is told from the point of view of a hearing person, and she is just now learning what it means to rely on reading lips, gestures, and body language, and how to communicate with a deaf child. And second, the story. I didn't want to draw too much attention to communication difficulties, but rather keep my focus on the crime, and how it impacts the boy, and the people around him.

MORE...

Victorian Mysteries:

Find all my books here:
www.anneliewendeberg.com

ACKNOWLEDGMENTS

A huge bear hug goes to the lovely people over at Silent-Witnesses.com who have supported the making of this book:

Gloria Horton-Young, Terry Webster, Caroline Wolfram, Rich Lovin, Bernadine Yeghoian, Michael Morrison, Victoria Dillman, Terry Kearns, Debby Avery, Walki Tinkanesh, Steve Howard, Tom Welch, Gudrun Thäter, Carry Pandya, Linda Stepp, Linda Koch, Nancy McDonald, Debra Powers, Shihlin Hsu, Maureen Carden, Nikkia Neil, Villia Jefremovas, and Carol Fusco.

And to my beta readers Magnus Wendeberg, Karen Entzming, Carol Tilsen, Kim Wright, Sabrina Flynn, Rich Lovin, and my ever-patient proofreader Tom Welch.

THANK YOU ALL!

88559623R00104